RESCUE

The Riverboat Adventures

1. *Escape Into the Night*
2. *Race for Freedom*
3. *Midnight Rescue*
4. *The Swindler's Treasure*

Adventures of the Northwoods

1. *The Disappearing Stranger*
2. *The Hidden Message*
3. *The Creeping Shadows*
4. *The Vanishing Footprints*
5. *Trouble at Wild River*
6. *The Mysterious Hideaway*
7. *Grandpa's Stolen Treasure*
8. *The Runaway Clown*
9. *Mystery of the Missing Map*
10. *Disaster on Windy Hill*

MIDNIGHT RESCUE

LOIS WALFRID JOHNSON

BETHANY HOUSE PUBLISHERS
MINNEAPOLIS, MINNESOTA 55438

18056

Midnight Rescue
Copyright © 1996
Lois Walfrid Johnson

Major David McKee, Benjamin Franklin Pearson, Dr. Edwin James, the
fugitive Dick, Dr. William Salter, Governor and Senator James Wilson
Grimes, and Colonel David Moore are historic characters who lived in the
1850s. The numerous escapes from the Minnesota Territorial Prison in
Stillwater are also a part of history. However, Sam McGrady and all other
characters are fictitious. Any resemblance to persons living or dead is
coincidental.

Cover illustration by Andrea Jorgenson
Story illustrations by Catherine McLaughlin
Side-wheeler illustration by Toni Auble
Map of Upper Mississippi by Meridian Mapping

Published by Bethany House Publishers
A Ministry of Bethany Fellowship, Inc.
11300 Hampshire Avenue South
Minneapolis, Minnesota 55438

Printed in the United States of America.

Library of Congress Cataloging-in-Publication Data

Johnson, Lois Walfrid.
    Midnight rescue / Lois Walfrid Johnson
        p.   cm. — (The riverboat adventures ; #3)
    Sequel to: Race for freedom.
    Summary: In 1857, having arrived in Minnesota Territory on her
father's steamboat, twelve-year-old Libby continues to harbor the
runaway slave boy Jordan while worrying about a fugitive who has
escaped from the local prison.
    ISBN 1-55661-353-9
    [1. Underground railroad—Fiction. 2. Fugitive slaves—Fiction.
3. Slavery—Fiction. 4. Afro-Americans—Fiction. 5. Steamboats—
Fiction. 6. Mississippi River—Fiction. 7. Prisoners—Fiction.
8. Christian life—Fiction.]
  I. Title. II. Series: Johnson, Lois Walfrid. Riverboat adventures ; #3.
    PZ7.J63255Mi   1996
[Fic]—dc20   96–45763   CIP
                                                             AC

To
Carol,
Martha and Ryan,
Charlotte,
Judy,
and
Nadine.

Thank you!

LOIS WALFRID JOHNSON is the bestselling author of more than twenty-six books. Her work has been translated into twelve languages and has received many awards, including the Gold Medallion, five Silver Angels, and the Wisconsin State Historical Society Award. Yet Lois believes that one of her greatest rewards is knowing that readers enjoy her books.

In her fun times she likes to camp, bike, cross-country ski, be with family and friends, and talk with young people like you. Lois and her husband, Roy, live in Minnesota.

In the time in which this book was set, African Americans were not known by that name. They were called *Negroes*, which is the Spanish word for black, or *colored people*.

The Native Americans in the Stillwater, Minnesota, area were called *Sioux* and *Chippewa*. Now the Sioux prefer to be called *Dakota* and many Chippewa are once again using the name of *Ojibwa* (Oh-JIB-wah).

Contents

1. Clink, Clank! 13
2. Big Trouble! 21
3. Friend Caleb 27
4. Libby Turns Detective 35
5. The Disappearing Cookies 41
6. Rope Tricks 50
7. Bad News 60
8. Jordan's New Plan 68
9. The Red Shirts 76
10. Peddler Paul 86
11. Family Spy 96
12. Nighttime Visit 107
13. Jordan's Signal 114
14. Bloodhounds! 123
15. The Fox River Outlaws 131
16. You Owes Me! 138
17. Dangerous Crossing 144
18. The Secret Stairway 154
19. Betrayed? 161
A Note From Lois 169
Acknowledgments 171

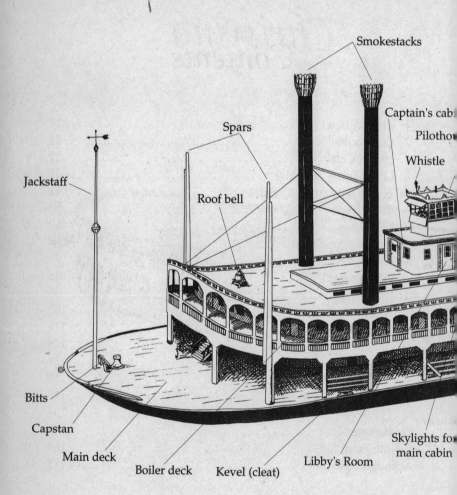

Smokestacks

Captain's cabi

Pilotho

Whistle

Spars

Jackstaff

Roof bell

Bitts

Capstan

Main deck

Boiler deck

Kevel (cleat)

Libby's Room

Skylights for
main cabin

The Side-wheeler Christina

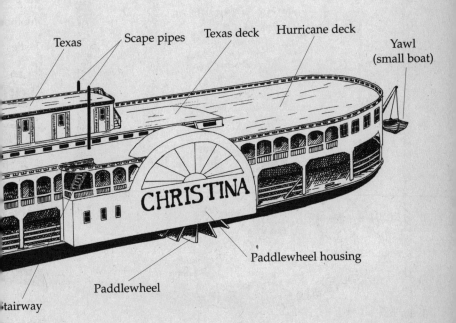

Texas   Scape pipes   Texas deck   Hurricane deck   Yawl (small boat)

CHRISTINA

Paddlewheel housing

Paddlewheel

Stairway

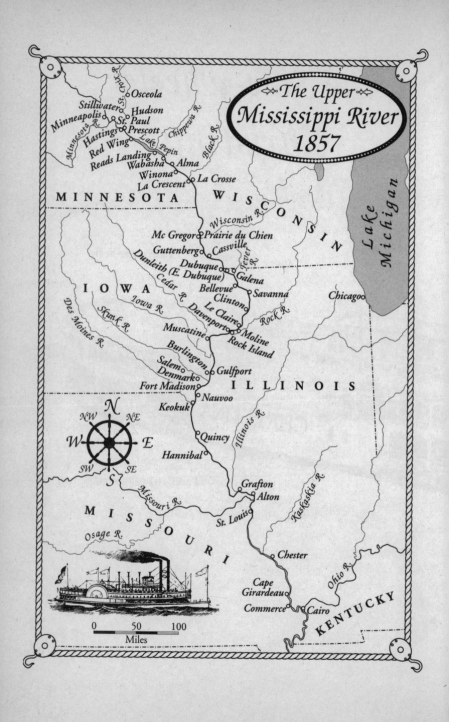

The Upper Mississippi River 1857

Osceola
Stillwater
Minneapolis
Hudson
St. Paul
Prescott
Hastings
Red Wing
Reads Landing
Wabasha
Alma
Winona
La Crescent
La Crosse

St. Croix R.
Minnesota R.
Chippewa R.
Lake Pepin
Black R.

MINNESOTA
WISCONSIN

Wisconsin R.

Mc Gregor
Prairie du Chien
Guttenberg
Cassville
Dunleith
(E. Dubuque)
Dubuque
Galena
Fever R.

IOWA

Bellevue
Clinton
Savanna
Le Claire
Davenport
Muscatine
Moline
Rock Island
Burlington
Salem
Denmark
Gulfport
Fort Madison
Keokuk
Nauvoo

Cedar R.
Iowa R.
Skunk R.
Des Moines R.
Rock R.

Chicago
Lake Michigan

ILLINOIS

Illinois R.

Quincy
Hannibal

N
NW NE
W   E
SW SE
S

Grafton
Alton
St. Louis

Missouri R.
Osage R.

MISSOURI

Kaskaskia R.

Chester

Cape
Girardeau
Commerce
Cairo
Ohio R.

KENTUCKY

0   50   100
Miles

1

Clink, Clank!

*T*he moment the whistle sounded, Libby Nor-
stad felt the excitement. From a deck high on the *Christina*, she
stared upstream. *Adventure! That's what this is. Living on Pa's steamboat
is an adventure! Every boy and girl I know would like to be where I am.*

As if something special were about to happen, Libby wished she
could tell the boat to hurry. Then she remembered. Danger had
chased them up the Mississippi River to Minnesota Territory. In the
darkness of night they had slipped away from St. Paul. Was that
same danger following them even now?

While the sun rose above the eastern bluffs, Libby's excitement
changed to uneasiness. "When does adventure become trouble?"
she asked her friend Caleb Whitney as he joined her at the railing.

Caleb snapped his fingers. "Just that quick!" he said.

At thirteen, Caleb was nearly a year older than Libby, but only an
inch taller. His blond hair fell down over his forehead, nearly reaching his eyes. "Stillwater is next," he said. "You'll like it there."

Just then the *Christina's* whistle sounded again. Long and deep,
the call broke the quiet of early morning. From shore a man's big
voice sang out, "Steamboat a-comin'!"

As the village of Stillwater came alive, people of all sizes and ages rushed toward the river. Boys and girls raced for a spot with the best view. Not far behind came mothers and fathers with younger children and babies in their arms. Everyone seemed to have one thought—reaching the riverfront before the steamboat tied up.

Soon only a narrow strip of water lay between the *Christina* and shore. As the crowd grew even larger, those in the back kept moving around, trying to see everything.

When a young boy called out from shore, Libby and Caleb waved to him. Soon the boy shouted a question. "Do you live on the boat?"

Caleb grinned down at him, enjoying the child's curiosity. "I'm a cabin boy," he shouted back. "Libby's father is the captain."

"Where did you come from?" a girl called.

"All the way from St. Louis. It's spring there. How come you don't have spring here?"

The grown-ups in the crowd laughed. Though it was the second week in May, 1857, the air was still cold. Everyone knew that Minnesota Territory had just come through one of the worst winters in its history.

"What's your cargo?" a man shouted.

"Cookstoves, sewing machines, and cloth for your ladies to make dresses," Caleb told them. "Axes, saws, and plows for you."

"And candy?" a small boy asked.

"Yup. Just the kind of candy you'll like."

As deckhands threw out the lines, eager people caught and held them. When the gangplank went down, the deckhands raced to tie the ropes to posts on shore.

Just then Libby heard the clip-clop of horses coming closer and closer. Soon a team and wagon swung around a building near the waterfront. A twelve- or thirteen-year-old boy sat on the high seat of the wagon. As his horses reached an open area, he called out, "Whoa!" Standing up, he leaped to the ground and tied a lead rope to the hitching rail.

When the boy reached the back of the crowd, he raised both arms and waved. "Hey, Caleb!" he shouted. "Over here!"

In the next moment Caleb spotted him. "Hi, Nate! Wait for me! I'll be right down!"

Caleb turned to Libby. "I met Nate the last time I was in Stillwater. Want to come with us? He'll take us around."

Without waiting for Libby's answer, Caleb headed for the stairs. "Help me find Jordan so he can go with us."

"Caleb?" Libby asked as she followed him down a flight of steps to the deck below. "Is it safe for Jordan to be seen in Stillwater?"

Only a short time before, Jordan Parker had run away from his master, a cruel slave trader named Riggs. Like Caleb, Jordan now worked for Libby's father as a cabin boy. Because of all that happened on their trip up the Mississippi River, Jordan had become known to everyone on the boat.

Caleb turned back to Libby. "He's as safe here as anywhere outside of Canada."

Libby caught Caleb's hidden meaning. "That's not very safe," she said.

"You're right." Caleb's honest gaze met hers. "We can't ever forget the fugitive slave laws. Wherever we go there might be someone who doesn't want Jordan to have his freedom. As long as even one person feels that way, Jordan will be in danger."

After a quick search of the boiler deck, Libby followed Caleb down another stairway. There had been more than one fugitive slave law. As part of the Compromise of 1850, Congress had strengthened the right of a slave owner to hunt down and capture fugitives, even in free northern states. Owners often hired catchers—rough, cruel men—to bring back runaway slaves.

On the main deck Caleb turned into the large open room for storing cargo. As they found their way between boxes and barrels, Libby asked, "What if the wrong person figures out that Jordan is a fugitive?"

"Shhh!" Only crew members were here, but Caleb glanced around to make sure no one was listening. "There will always be people who want the big reward offered for Jordan. But he can't spend his whole life being scared."

As Caleb passed the opening to a secret hiding place, he didn't even glance that way. "We can't let anything stop Jordan now. He's figured out a perfect plan to rescue his family."

"A safe plan?" Libby asked.

"The safest that something so dangerous can be."

"Can I go along?" Libby asked. With every part of her being she wanted to help Jordan's family escape to freedom.

"Maybe," Caleb said.

Libby's heart leaped. *Caleb said maybe.* Since the age of nine, he had worked with the Underground Railroad—the secret plan that helped slaves escape to freedom. Always before when Libby asked if she could take part in the rescue, Caleb had said no. If he said *maybe*, he might mean *yes*!

But then Caleb told her, "It's up to Jordan whether or not you go. It's going to be a hard trip. We can't give away even one secret."

Lifting her head, Libby tossed her long red hair. *So! I'll prove that I can help rescue Jordan's family. For a start, I'll show Caleb and Jordan that I can keep a secret.*

When Libby and Caleb passed through another door, they found Jordan in the engine room. Tall and strong, the runaway slave was about thirteen or fourteen years old.

Libby, Caleb, and Jordan hurried outside and down the gangplank. Along the riverfront, people greeted one another as if they had been separated for years.

Near Libby a little girl leaped into her daddy's arms. An older man shook hands with someone who seemed to have been gone on business. A young woman gazed up into the eyes of a handsome young man. When he smiled down at her, Libby felt the quick stab of memory. *That's the way Pa used to look at Ma.*

Libby pushed the thought away, not wanting loneliness for her mother to spoil the sunshine of the day. Always Libby felt glad she could be with Pa again after the four years she lived in Chicago because of Ma's death.

When Libby and the boys reached Nate, he stood near his wagon, waiting for them. As Caleb introduced Libby and Jordan, Nate caught Libby's last name. "Your pa is the captain?" he asked. "Heard your whistle way out at our farm."

He turned to Caleb. "I knew you were back again."

"By the sound of the whistle?" Libby felt pleased.

"Yup, clear and deep. I like your bell too. It's one of the best on the river."

Nate couldn't possibly have said anything nicer. Always Libby had been proud of the *Christina*'s bell. More than once, her father had told Libby how it was made. When the bell was being cast, its makers threw silver dollars into the bronze to give a silvery tone.

"Pa sent me to pick up the plow we ordered from the general store," Nate explained. "We've got time before it's unloaded, don't we?"

Caleb nodded. "The freight we brought from St. Louis is down in the hold."

"Want a ride to see the town?" Nate grinned. "Of all the people in Stillwater I'm the very best one to take you around. I'll show you the most fun places in the whole St. Croix Valley."

The *Saint Kroy* River flowed between Minnesota Territory and the state of Wisconsin. The village of Stillwater was built at the head of the widening in the river called *Lake St. Croix*.

As Nate went forward to untie the lead rope, he walked around the horses, talking to both Tom and Bob and checking their harness. Then Nate and Jordan climbed up to the only seat, and Caleb helped Libby into the back of the wagon.

Because of the large wheels, the bed of the wagon was about three feet off the ground. Instead of sitting down, Libby and Caleb stood behind Nate and Jordan to see over the high sides of the wagon.

"Giddyup!" Nate called to Tom and Bob, and the horses moved out into the road.

A short distance from the waterfront Nate turned onto a street with tall wooden buildings. Caleb looked up a steep hill on their left.

"There's Nelson's Grade!" he exclaimed. "That's where you took me before. Want to go again?"

Nate shook his head. "Someone just had a bad accident there. I'll show you the view from a better hill."

On Main Street the dirt road was filled with mud. As the horses picked their way around large holes, the wagon jerked and bounced in the ruts. Libby grabbed the high board sides and hung on.

"Have you lived here long?" she asked Nate.

"All my life."

"You must know these hills really well," Libby said.

"Yup. Lots of caves in 'em. There are caves even in the bluff surrounding Battle Hollow."

"What's Battle Hollow?" Libby was curious.

"I'll show you. It's a hollowed-out place with steep rock walls. There was a big battle there between the Sioux and Chippewa Indians. That's where the prison for Minnesota Territory is now."

Soon Nate turned left onto a street with a gentle rise. A block farther on, the horses turned again, and the bed of the wagon took on a sharp slant. As Tom and Bob leaned into their harness, Libby shifted her feet to keep her balance.

The road ahead was long and steep and followed the edge of a straight-up-and-down bluff. On the right side, the ground dropped sharply away with only a few large rocks between the edge of the road and the drop-off. With most of the trees cut off the hillsides, Libby had a clear view in whatever direction she looked.

The higher they went, the greater the distance between the top and the bottom of the bluff. Seventy-five? One hundred feet? Libby wasn't sure. She only knew that she felt scared just looking down.

Again Libby braced her feet and clung to the sides of the wagon. To her relief the boards were chest high, giving more protection than usual. But none of the boys seemed to share Libby's concern. She could only hope that Caleb didn't see how frightened she felt.

I never knew that heights would bother me so much, Libby thought. *I'm glad we're going up, not down*. Then she remembered. *What goes up must come down*.

Trying to take her mind off the steep drop, Libby asked Nate about the prison.

"Built from a quarry right here in Stillwater," Nate said proudly. "Trouble is, it doesn't keep prisoners in. Just last year eight of 'em escaped."

"Eight?" Jordan asked, as if thinking about his own escape. "How did they git out?"

"It ain't hard at all," Nate said. "One prisoner pried up the floor in a hall. Another lifted a cell door from its hinges. Still another used a burglar's bar."

"Smuggled in, I bet," Caleb said.

Nate's eyes were full of laughter. "Another prisoner sawed through iron window bars. And one guy picked the locks on his chains. Someone else dug a hole through the outside wall."

"There must be something really wrong," Caleb said.

Nate grinned. "To my way of thinking the warden just lets 'em go."

"Are you serious?" Libby asked. "How could someone who is supposed to keep prisoners locked up just let them go?"

Nate shrugged. "Some of the counties don't pay money to feed their prisoners. We even had a lady escape."

"Aw, c'mon," Libby said, not sure what she should believe.

Nate held up his right hand. "The whole truth, and nothing but the truth. It's as plain as the hair on your head who those prisoners are. Just last week I saw one of them."

"On the loose?" Libby didn't like the idea of an escaped prisoner running around. What if one of them tried to board the *Christina*?

But Nate seemed to have no such dread. "I saw the prisoner down by the river. Half of his hair was the way it should be."

Libby's giggle sounded more nervous than she would like. "What do you mean—half of his hair?" She felt sure that Nate was teasing them. "You're making things up."

"Nothing funny about it." Nate looked offended now. "Half of his hair looked just like mine—about the same length. The other half of his head was shaved clean."

Libby couldn't even imagine it.

"Not one speck of hair on that side," Nate said. "That's how you know who a prisoner is."

"Do they wear uniforms?" Caleb asked.

"Wel-l-l-l—" Nate thought about it. "They all wear the same thing—gray pants, a shirt, jacket, and cap. But the best way to recognize a prisoner is by his haircut."

Libby's knuckles were white now from holding the top board of the wagon. The sharp drop at the edge of the bluff was so close to the wheels that it made her nervous. If she had her way about things, she would get out of the wagon and walk.

When the road finally leveled out, Libby felt relieved. At the top of the bluff Nate stopped the horses. He was right about one thing. There couldn't be a better view anywhere.

Gazing upstream and down, Libby watched the sunlight dance upon the water. Here at the head of Lake St. Croix masses of logs floated like large islands. Across the lake, sandstone bluffs rose high and beautiful.

Libby caught her breath at the beauty. Far below, men hurried up and down the *Christina*'s gangplank, unloading her cargo. Between the boat and Libby, houses clung to the steep hillside.

Like Libby, Caleb and Jordan studied the great stretch of water

before them. It wasn't hard to guess what they were searching for—
a steamboat that might bring news about the two-hundred-dollar
reward offered for Jordan.

Then, as Libby feared, Caleb stretched out his arm, pointing
downstream. "Steamboat a-comin'," he said.

Still far away, small plumes of black smoke rose from two tall
stacks. It was a steamboat all right. Which one? And who was
aboard? People who had never heard of Jordan? Or his enemies?

When Caleb and Jordan looked at each other, Libby felt sure she
knew what they were thinking. Only then did she realize how
much she dreaded having the wrong person follow Jordan because
he was a fugitive.

As Nate drove on, he stopped the horses on the bluff behind the
territorial prison. Here too, the hill in front of them was stripped
bare of trees. Libby looked down across the roofs of three-story
high buildings that stretched away toward the river.

On the back and two sides the bluff formed a natural hollow
around the prison. On Libby's left, the bluff was straight-up-and-
down rock. Directly below her and the boys, the steep hill slanted
more gradually away. Between the bottom of the bluff and the
buildings was a twelve-foot stone wall.

As Nate pointed toward the warden's house, a clank broke the
stillness of the morning.

What is it? Libby gazed down into the hollow, trying to figure
out where the sound came from. In the prison yard everything
seemed to be as it had been.

Then Libby heard a second clank—the sound of metal against
metal. This time she noticed a pipe railing around the top of the
prison wall. Below where she stood something hung from the pipe.

Staring down, Libby decided it was a large hook. A rope hung
from the hook, dropping inside the prison wall. While Libby
watched, the rope stretched tight.

"Look!" she whispered to Caleb. The rope swayed now, swinging out away from the wall as if someone was climbing up. "A prisoner is trying to escape!"

In the next instant a hand reached up to where the rope showed
above the wall. Another hand grasped the pipe, and a half-shaved
head appeared.

2

Big Trouble!

$\mathcal{A}$s Libby and the boys watched, a man pulled himself up, then swung a leg over the wall.

"I bet the warden went to see the *Christina* come in," Nate muttered.

For a moment the prisoner balanced on top of the wall. With quick movements he pulled up the rope, yanked the hook free, and dropped the rope outside the wall.

Libby leaned forward, trying for a better look at his face. Just then the prisoner turned. As he grasped the pipe railing with both hands, Libby saw the bundle on his back. Swinging his legs free, the prisoner touched down on the steep hill close to the top of the wall.

As he picked up the rope, he glanced around, then up the bluff to where Libby and the boys waited in the wagon. Suddenly the man jerked back. As if trying to hide his face, he ducked his head. Grabbing bushes and weeds for a handhold, he crept along the side of the hill.

"We've got to get help!" Caleb exclaimed.

"It's a hard climb," Nate said as if doubting the man could get out.

"Right here the hill is slanted enough for him to make it," Caleb answered. "He'll get away."

"Not if we hurry." In the narrow road Nate turned the horses sharply, then backed up. The moment Tom and Bob completed the turn, Nate slapped the reins across their backs.

"Giddyup!" he cried. As the horses swung around a curve, they picked up speed. Soon they reached the level ground at the top of the long steep hill. As Libby looked ahead, her fear of heights returned.

On her right, the ground at the side of the road rose upward. On her left, the bluff fell away to nothing. Remembering the frightening drop to the ground far below, Libby felt her stomach turn over. *If the harness holds. If nothing goes wrong—*

As they started down the long hill, Nate pulled back on the reins. When the horses slowed to a walk, Libby felt relieved. As if digging in their rear hooves, Tom and Bob held back the weight of the wagon.

Nate spoke to them now. "Good boys. Easy—that's the way."

Breathing deeply, Libby felt almost silly. *Here I was so scared for no reason at all.* For a moment she glanced toward the river, almost enjoying the view.

In the next instant everything changed. As the steep hill forced the harness forward, the wagon lurched. Libby rocked back. Tightening her grip, she clung to the high wooden sides of the wagon. Standing next to Libby, Caleb braced his feet and hung on.

Again the wagon lurched. Suddenly the horses started running.

"Whoa!" Nate called, pulling back on the reins. Instead, Tom and Bob picked up their speed.

"Whoa!" Nate cried again.

When Bob tossed his head, Libby saw the terror in his eyes. Fighting against the harness, Tom veered off to the right and the rising hill. Then Bob pulled left, and the wagon swayed. As the horses moved into a gallop, Libby's heart pounded. The horses were running away!

"Whoa!" Leaning back, Nate pulled at the reins, but nothing happened. "Whoa!" he called again. Instead, the wheels went faster and faster.

Suddenly Jordan reached over, grabbing the reins. His hands

next to Nate's, they pulled together. With all their strength they hung on. But there was no stopping the horses. On the narrow road the wagon rocked dangerously.

Just then Jordan leaped from the high front seat. Hitting the ground in a ball, he rolled, picked himself up, and raced after the horses. But the wagon swung past him, so close that the rear wheel almost hit him.

Filled with terror, Libby stared down over the high wood sides. The boards that had seemed to protect her now made it impossible to leap.

Libby whirled around. When she tried to walk toward the open back end, she staggered. Unable to move against the slant of the wagon, she almost fell.

Her panic growing, Libby grabbed the sides of the wagon again. As she faced forward, Tom veered to the right. Bob again pulled left. Rocking from side to side, the wagon swung out of control. Moments later, the horses headed straight for a big rock on the edge of the bluff.

From next to Libby, Caleb shouted, "Get down!"

Instead, Libby froze, unable to let go. Grabbing her arm, Caleb pushed her to the floor of the wagon. "Cover your head!"

Still frozen by terror, Libby had time for only one thought. *What will Pa do without me?*

Then arms came down on top of her head. The wagon wobbled, then tipped. As a horse screamed, the wagon rolled on its side. With a great lurch and cracking wood, it slammed to a stop.

When a second horse snorted, Libby shuddered. Without moving, she tried to figure out where she was. *The steep road. The wagon. The runaway horses.*

Then she remembered. *Caleb told me to get down.*

As Libby stirred and tried to look up, she saw Caleb's arms protecting her head.

"You okay, Libby?" he asked. Moving slowly, he sat back on his heels.

Again Libby stirred. *Am I okay?* she wondered.

She wiggled her toes. Yes, she could feel them. Her legs, her arms, and her hands all seemed to work. But Libby felt dazed. Why was she kneeling on the side instead of the bottom of the wagon? The wagon tilted strangely too.

Still feeling odd, Libby looked up into Caleb's scared eyes. "Are *you* okay?" she asked.

Caleb nodded, but when Libby tried to move, he stopped her. "We're at the edge of the bluff," he warned. "There's only a rock holding us."

"One rock? A big one?" Again terror filled Libby, reaching through her dazed feelings.

"The horses headed straight for it," Caleb said. "Bob went to one side and Tom to the other. They broke the pole, and the wagon swung around."

"Out over the edge?" Libby could barely speak.

Caleb nodded. "Don't move," he warned again.

"Jordan?" Libby asked, remembering. Jordan had jumped free, trying to catch the horses.

"I can't see him," Caleb said. "I don't dare look."

"Nate?" Libby felt afraid to even breathe. As though able to see the steep drop below them, she remembered.

"I don't know," Caleb said.

Then Libby heard Jordan's voice. "Hold still," he warned as Caleb had.

Barely moving her head, Libby looked around. This time she understood what she saw. The wagon lay on its side with ground beneath the smashed front boards. The back end of the wagon hung at a crazy angle over the edge of the bluff. The only way out was through the open top, which was half on and half off the bluff.

Between the broken front boards Libby could see Jordan. "We got to unhitch the horses before they shake everything loose," he said.

Jordan was gone then, and Libby heard him talking quietly, soothing the horses. Through the splintered wood she heard a second voice, then saw Nate working to free the horses. Tom stood on one side of the large rock, Bob on the other, only a few feet from the edge of the bluff.

"Nate jumped off too?" Libby asked.

"Or was thrown," Caleb told her. "I don't know which. I was just thinking about you."

"And my head." Libby tried to smile, but her lips felt stiff. "Thanks, Caleb. Are you sure *your* head is okay?"

"My head is okay," Caleb said.

"And the rest of you?" Libby asked.

"We both got down in time. The high sides protected us."

For what seemed forever they waited, neither of them moving. Now and then they heard a whinny, as though the horses were still terrified.

"What happened?" Libby finally asked. Her voice was soft, as if even the sound could break the wagon free.

"Something spooked the horses," Caleb said. "Whatever it was, I knew Nate wouldn't be able to stop them. And we wouldn't be able to get out."

Always Libby felt amazed at how quickly Caleb figured out what to do. "You knew all that in the midst of horses running away?"

Then Libby remembered. "That man climbing over the wall. The escaped prisoner must have gotten away."

"Afraid so," Caleb answered.

"He scares me," Libby said. "He really scares me." Forgetting where she was, Libby moved. As the wagon shifted, her stomach bottomed out. Then the wagon settled again.

After what seemed like ages, Jordan dropped the end of a lead rope over what had been the side of the wagon. "You needs to hang on to this so we can help you out," he said.

Caleb gave the rope to Libby. "Tie it around under your arms," he said.

With shaking fingers Libby knotted the rope. When she was ready, Jordan spoke again.

"Take it slow and easylike," he said. "Me and Nate is holdin' the rope, but you got to crawl out."

"You first, Libby," Caleb said. "Stay on your hands and knees."

The moment she moved, Jordan and Nate tightened the rope. As Libby crawled across the boards that had been the side of the wagon, her full, ankle-length skirt caught on a splinter. When she freed the cloth, she moved into the opening. There she took one look down.

Only two feet beyond where she knelt, the ground dropped

away to nothing. Far below, the houses seemed like tiny toy buildings.

Libby's muscles tightened. Forcing herself to move on, she set down her right hand. Just beyond her fingers, the ground crumbled, then gave way. When she heard pebbles land far below, Libby again froze.

"Keep movin'," Jordan told her. The rope tightened around her, but Libby could not pick up her hand.

"Put your right knee forward," Caleb said from behind. But fear held Libby as if the rope were pulling her back instead of forward.

His voice calm and steady, Caleb spoke again. "Put your right knee forward."

This time Libby could move.

"Bring up your left knee," Caleb told her.

Again Libby obeyed. Movement by movement, Caleb told her what to do.

"Keep going," Caleb encouraged her whenever she hesitated. "You're almost there."

At last Libby crawled around the front of the wagon to the solid ground where Jordan and Nate stood.

The moment Libby untied the rope, Jordan returned it to Caleb. Her knees still weak with fright, Libby sank down on safe ground. Her arms were shaking, and her teeth chattered with nervousness.

As soon as Caleb said he was ready, Jordan and Nate drew the rope tight. Bracing their feet, they called to Caleb. "C'mon out!"

Through the broken pieces of wood at the front of the wagon, Libby saw Caleb's head. The instant he moved, the wagon shifted. Pulling hard on the rope, Jordan and Nate stepped back.

Again Caleb edged forward. Again the wagon shifted. Dirt and small stones slid out from beneath the boards and rained down the side of the bluff.

Libby leaped to her feet. Filled with panic, she cried out, "Caleb!"

3

Friend Caleb

Only a foot of dirt remained between the front of the wagon and the edge of the bluff. Again Jordan and Nate moved back, bracing their feet on solid ground.

Standing behind Nate, Libby took up the end of the rope. With all three of them hanging on, Caleb crawled out on the narrow strip of ground. Moments later he reached safety.

Only then did Libby draw a deep breath of relief. When she looked around, she saw the horses farther down the road. Instead of a lead rope, reins stretched between them and a tree. No longer able to run, Bob tossed his head, his eyes still wild with fear.

Like a matchstick, the pole at the front of the wagon was broken into pieces. The front boards were also shattered beyond use. Seeing them, Libby remembered Nate. "Did you jump?" she asked him.

He nodded. "About two seconds before we hit."

Just then Libby saw people coming from all directions to help them. While some of the men rubbed down the sweating horses, others worked together to turn the wagon upright. When they found that two of the wheels still rolled, they pushed the wagon across the road, lodging it against the upward side of the bluff.

With Nate leading the horses, Libby and the boys once more started toward the riverfront. They had walked only a few steps when a farmer stopped to ask if everyone was all right. As soon as Nate tied the lead rope for his horses to the end of the farmer's wagon, he climbed up to the high seat. Libby, Caleb, and Jordan sat down in the back.

Leaning against the wooden side, Libby covered her eyes with her hands. She wanted to blot out all memory of the runaway horses. Yet, even with her eyes closed, she saw them again. Just thinking about their frantic race down the steep hill, Libby began to shake. *I never want to ride in a wagon again!*

Then, as she felt the boards beneath her, Libby knew she was doing just that. Embarrassed by her weakness, she forced herself to look up. "What happened?" she asked Jordan.

"The hold back broke," he said.

"The hold back?" Libby didn't know what he was talking about.

"A strap," Jordan explained. "It keeps the neck yoke tight to the horse."

"The neck yoke broke too?" Maybe that was one of the lurches she felt.

"Yes'm. The wagon started runnin' up on the horses. The single-trees—"

"Singletree?" Libby was lost again.

"A crossbar behind each horse," Caleb said quickly. "They're part of the wagon."

Jordan grinned. "When them singletrees start slappin' against them horses' heels, whoo-ee! Them horses spooked!"

Libby wasn't sure she understood it all. Already she felt her bruises, but she also felt grateful that she was alive. Still, she was curious. "Jordan, how do you know so much about horses?"

Jordan straightened and lifted his head in the proud look Libby had come to know. "That's why I has value," he said.

"Value?"

Jordan glanced toward Nate and the farmer. When he spoke, his voice was low. "That's why I is worth a big reward. I knows more about horses than any other colored boy I know."

"Is that right, Jordan?" Even Caleb looked surprised. "How did you learn?"

"Before my daddy got sold away he taught me. He said, 'Jordan, you listen up now. You learn everything I teach you 'cause if you has value you has an easier life.' "

Jordan shook his head. "Someday when I git my family free, I is goin' to prove my value. I is goin' to show my daddy how much he taught me."

"I thought you didn't know where he is," Libby said.

"I ain't got no idea where he is. But when Momma and my sisters and my brother is free, I is goin' to find him."

The moment they reached downtown Stillwater, Caleb hunted up the village marshall to report the escaped prisoner. The marshall was glad Caleb had told him. Yet he shook his head at still another escape.

When Libby and the boys returned to the waterfront, they found the steamboat they had seen from the top of the bluff. A smaller boat than the *Christina*, it was the kind that usually traveled up and down the St. Croix River. They had no way of knowing if it had gone into St. Paul. Nor could they tell if the boat had picked up passengers who might know the latest news and remember Jordan.

When it was time to say goodbye, Nate grinned at Libby. "If you come back to Stillwater, I'll give you another ride," he said.

As Libby shuddered, Nate's eyes grew serious. "I'm sorry, Libby. Really sorry about what happened."

Only then could Libby smile. "It was a great view, Nate. Thanks for trying. I know it wasn't your fault."

"Next time I'll take better care of you," he promised.

As Libby looked up, she saw Caleb watching them.

When Libby went on board the *Christina*, her dog, Samson, met her at the top of the gangplank. A big black Newfoundland, he had white patches on his nose, muzzle, chest, and the tips of his toes. Dropping down on her knees, Libby give him a big hug.

As if he sensed that she needed comfort, Samson reached out his long tongue and tried to lick her. Though Libby edged away from his slobbering, she felt better.

Soon the *Christina* put out into Lake St. Croix. As the boat steamed upstream, Libby, Caleb, and Jordan watched from the main deck. The water was crowded with the logs Libby had seen from the bluff.

Two miles above the village, lumbermen had built a large boom—a barrier made of a chain of floating logs. Stretched between long islands and the high bluffs on both sides of the river, the boom caught logs coming down the St. Croix River. Once collected, these logs were measured and sorted according to the owner's mark on the end of each log.

Some of these logs went to a Stillwater sawmill. Others floated downstream in rafts.

In the open water below the boom, men balanced on the spinning logs. Wearing boots with sharp spikes in the sole and heel, each of them held a long pole called a *pike*. Its point tapered down into a two-inch thread that looked like a screw. Using the pikes, the men guided the logs into long strings that would then be made into rafts.

"Why are all the men wearing red shirts?" Libby asked.

"If a man falls into the river, it's easier to see him in a red shirt," Caleb explained.

Soon the *Christina* nosed into the riverbank below the boom. On the sandstone bluff above the boat was a large cookhouse where the Red Shirts had their meals. According to Caleb, the cooks often fed six hundred men a day.

In the side of the bluff and below the cookhouse was a cave used to store food and supplies. The minute the *Christina*'s gangplank went down, roustabouts started unloading cargo. As the laborers carried supplies into the cave, Libby hurried up to the hurricane deck. There she knelt down at her favorite spot for watching what was going on. From behind the railing she could see the front part of the main deck, though two decks below.

As Samson dropped down beside her, Libby ran her fingers through the long hair at the back of his neck. When she scratched behind his ears, Samson's mouth stretched wide, as though trying to smile. Again he seemed to sense how shaky Libby still felt.

One moment Libby felt glad for the way Caleb had watched out for her. The next moment she trembled just thinking about how close they had come to the edge of the bluff. It reminded Libby of the important promise she had made only a few days before. Going beyond all her fears, she had asked God for His love and forgiveness.

Now Libby clutched that memory to herself. *If something had happened to me, I would have been ready to die.*

Sitting there on the deck, Libby felt even more grateful to the God she was learning to know in a deeper way. "Thanks for protecting me," Libby prayed softly. "Thanks for watching over all of us."

Everything had happened so fast, she had almost forgotten about the escaped prisoner. Even Caleb's promise that *maybe* she could help rescue Jordan's family had slipped to the back of her mind. Now it became real again. *Maybe I will be able to help when Jordan tries to rescue his family! I'll prove I can keep a secret—that I can do whatever I set out to do!*

Then an uneasy thought sneaked into Libby's mind. *Can I really do anything I set out to do?* Remembering her close call on the bluff, Libby felt shaky again. *Helpless, that's what I was. As helpless as a baby.*

Pushing the memory away, she refused to think about it. *I'm a Christian now. Life will be easier.*

Just then Libby noticed a man coming down the steps from the cookhouse. As though he knew exactly where he was going, he hurried across a sandy piece of ground to the *Christina*. When he reached the gangplank, he spoke to the clerk standing nearby.

"Caleb Whitney?" the man asked. "Can I talk to him?"

Uh-oh, Libby thought. *What's gone wrong now?*

Then she remembered Jordan. Had someone found out that he was a fugitive? Did someone know that Caleb had helped Jordan come aboard? Grown-ups were fined or put in prison for helping runaway slaves. The penalty was high, the risk great.

Lying down on her stomach, Libby peered between the posts of the railing. Before long Caleb crossed the forward deck to speak to the man.

"Caleb Whitney?" he asked again.

Instantly Caleb stiffened as if he too wondered what this was all about. But his back was toward Libby, and she couldn't see his face.

"I'm Caleb," she heard him say. "What can I do for you?"

Though Libby tried hard, she couldn't hear the man's answer.

After a few minutes Caleb led him up the gangplank. Near the front of the boat they sat down on two crates.

Now Libby could see Caleb's face, but it still didn't tell her anything. More than once she had noticed how good Caleb was about hiding his feelings. The bigger the danger, the better he seemed to be at not giving away one wrong expression or word.

Finally Libby could no longer push aside her curiosity. On her hands and knees, she backed away from the railing. Once out of Caleb's sight, Libby stood up and headed for the stairs. One flight down she came to the boiler deck, which was just above the large boiler that heated water and created steam to run the boat.

The next flight down was the main deck. There Libby walked toward the bow as if she were a passenger minding her own business. Pretending that she didn't know Caleb, she passed close by. Sitting down on a barrel, she looked out at the river.

"And the young lady's name?" the man asked.

The young lady? Libby wondered. *Who's he talking about?* Turning slightly, she watched the man write on a piece of paper.

"Libby Norstad," Caleb answered. "You should talk with her. She's quite a bright girl—most of the time, that is."

"That's all right. I'll just talk with you," the man said.

"You're sure? It would take just a minute to find her."

"Do you know her well?" the man asked.

"I work for her father," Caleb said. "I'm a cabin boy on the *Christina.*"

And so much more, Libby thought. Once Pa had told her how much Caleb meant to him. *"I'd trust him even with my life,"* Pa had said. Often Caleb helped Pa by hiding fugitive slaves.

In moments like this Libby had a hard time understanding the kind of trust Pa had for Caleb. Other times, such as during the wagon accident, she understood perfectly. More than once Caleb had done things that Libby admired. But this wasn't to be one of those times.

"I'll get Libby for you," Caleb said again. "You really need to talk to her."

"Why don't you tell me about her instead?" the man asked.

"Wel-l-l-l—" Caleb paused, as though hardly knowing where to begin. "Often she leaps before she looks. Does things I can't un-

derstand. Like listening in on other people's conversations. In fact, she listens in so often that I wonder if her ears will begin standing out on her head."

"Indeed?" the man said. "And why is she so curious?"

"I've often thought about that," Caleb answered. "I believe it has to do with her nature. She wants to know everything that is going on."

"If I ever see this young lady, how will I recognize her?"

From behind the man's back, Libby glared at Caleb. When their gaze met, she had no doubt that Caleb had seen her. For a moment she thought he was going to give her away. Instead, he kept looking at Libby while still talking to the man.

"Her nose is turned up just a bit," Caleb said. "Brown eyes. Deep brown eyes. You know, the kind of eyes your favorite dog might have.

"And red hair," Caleb went on. "Her hair is deep red with a bit of gold in it. Not bad at all, when the sun shines on it."

By now Libby's face felt hot with embarrassment. Whirling around, she tried to hide how she felt from Caleb. How could that awful boy do such a thing? She wanted to storm up to him, to tell him to mind his own business. Instead, she could only stomp off.

"I mean it. You really should talk to her," Caleb said as she started away. "Libby might tell you a whole other side of the story. For one thing she's afraid of heights. As we rode up the hill, she clung to the side of the wagon, as if terrified."

Who is this man Caleb is talking to? With all her heart Libby wanted to find out.

Then with horror she decided that she knew. *He must be a newspaper reporter!*

4

Libby Turns Detective

The minute the man was gone, Libby stomped up to Caleb. Already she had forgotten how he protected her in the accident. Instead, she felt embarrassed just thinking about what Caleb had said.

"And who was that gentleman you were talking to?" Libby asked sweetly.

Caleb's answer sounded just as innocent. "He's the reporter from the local newspaper. He wanted to know what we knew about the escaped prisoner. And he wanted to know about our accident."

"And you told him all about it," Libby said, her voice still sweet.

"Yup." Caleb sounded as if it weren't important. "He said there has already been a bad accident on Nelson's Grade—the road where Nate didn't want to take us. The reporter expects the town leaders will do something about railings on the drop-offs."

"And did you tell the reporter that Jordan was with us?" Libby couldn't forget her fear about what might happen.

"Nope," Caleb answered. "I didn't say a word about Jordan."

"But you said lots of words about me. Why did you talk to that man?"

"Why not?" Caleb asked. "I didn't tell him anything that he shouldn't know."

"So he should know *everything* you told him about me?"

"Yup." Caleb grinned.

Libby groaned. "That article will tell the whole world that the *Christina* came to Stillwater. When does the newspaper come out?"

"Once a week," Caleb said. "It comes out tomorrow, but not till after we leave."

"If someone buys that newspaper and carries it onto a steamboat going downstream—" Libby broke off. By now she felt so upset she could barely speak. Caleb had told *her* she needed to keep a secret. But was he doing it himself?

"You wanted to talk to that reporter because you want to be a reporter yourself," Libby went on.

"That's right," Caleb answered calmly.

"But what if the reporter talks to Nate? What if Nate tells him about Jordan? What if Jordan's name gets in the paper?"

Caleb groaned. "What if, what if, what if—"

Finally Libby had to give up. Nothing she could say would convince Caleb that he had done anything wrong.

Only then did Libby remember. She had forgotten to ask Caleb another really important question. "Did you find out more about the escaped prisoner?" she asked.

"His name is Sam," Caleb told her. "Sam McGrady. He went to prison for being part of a gang that robbed banks."

As the moon rose above the sandstone bluffs, Libby returned to her room high on the texas deck. Long after she went to bed, Libby tossed and turned. Wherever her arms and legs touched the mattress, she felt a new bruise. Until then she hadn't realized how much she bounced around when the wagon rolled on its side.

After a while Libby got up and tightened the ropes that stretched lengthwise and across her bed frame. Yet when she crawled back into bed, the corn husks in her mattress rustled whenever she turned over.

Now that she was past the first shock of the accident, her thoughts kept returning to the escaped prisoner. After learning about him, Captain Norstad had ordered the *Christina* a short distance out from shore. To protect passengers and freight, the *Christina*'s gangplank was up and a guard posted to watch throughout the night.

In the wee hours of morning, Libby gave up trying to sleep. Quickly she changed into her dress. Her room had two doors, one on either side of the boat. Without making a sound, Libby opened the door on the side away from where Samson always slept.

When Libby tiptoed out on deck, the night air was warm and sweet with the spring that had finally come. For a moment Libby listened to the night sounds. Then, walking on tiptoes, she took the few steps down to the hurricane deck. There Libby dropped onto her knees behind the railing.

Here in the quiet water below the boom site, Libby heard only the gentle lapping of waves against the shore. Soon her eyes grew used to the darkness. Between the boat and a nearby island, logs filled the river. Only between the *Christina* and shore was there a dark line of open water.

From somewhere on the main deck a baby cried, then was quiet again. From near the same area came loud snoring. After several minutes, Libby heard an *omooopf!* as if someone poked the person who snored.

Then to Libby's ears came a soft splash, and another. Instantly alert, she peered down over the railing. Near the shore she saw a shape darker than water.

Again Libby heard a muffled splash. As the shape moved closer, Libby strained to see. Whoever it was had either a very big head or wore a strangely shaped hat.

Then, as Libby watched, an arm reached out. In water still cold from winter, someone was swimming toward the *Christina*.

As her sense of danger came alive, Libby jumped to her feet and raced to the stairs. From the hurricane, to the boiler, to the main deck she flew. Stumbling over legs and feet in the darkness, she made her way to the side of the boat nearest shore. But she was too late.

When Libby stared down at the water only a foot or so below the deck, no one swam toward the *Christina*. No hands reached forward for a man to pull himself onto the deck.

Then Libby saw the guard. As he sat on a crate close to where the gangplank usually went down, his head seemed to nod. When Libby walked over to him, his head jerked up.

For an instant Libby wondered why the lantern wasn't lit. Had the guard just wakened? Libby wasn't sure.

"Can I help you, miss?" the man asked, seeming alert.

"Yes," Libby answered softly, trying not to wake the sleeping passengers around her. "Can you tell me if a man just came on board?"

"A man? Of course not. It's the middle of the night."

"No one at all?" Libby asked.

"Not for some time. All's well on the *Christina*."

"Thank you," Libby said. "And your name?"

"Swenson, Miss. Charlie Swenson, at your service."

Strange, Libby thought as she crept back up the stairs. *I was sure I saw a man swimming toward the Christina. But if I did, I should have seen him on deck. He couldn't have been more than a minute or two ahead of me.*

All the way back to her room Libby thought about it. Still fully dressed, she lay down on her bed to puzzle it out.

I'll go down there again, she decided. *As soon as it's light, I'll go back.* Minutes later Libby fell asleep.

Libby woke to the motion of the boat under way. For a minute she lay there, listening to the throb of the engines and the slap of the great paddle wheels against the water. As she came fully awake, she remembered the dark shape swimming toward the *Christina*.

With a bound Libby leaped from her bed. Quickly she poured water from the pitcher into the basin in the corner of her room. As soon as she splashed water on her face and smoothed down her dress, she was ready.

This time she went out on the side of the deck where Samson usually slept. As she flew down the flights of stairs, Samson trailed along behind her. All around Libby, passengers were waking up. Even so, Libby moved quickly through any narrow space between them.

At the crate next to where the gangplank usually went down, Libby stopped. Here the guard had sat. Here Libby had wondered if his head had nodded—if he was truly awake. There was something about the guard that bothered her. What was it?

Standing there, Libby's thoughts leaped back to the swimmer. A large hat. Why would someone wear a hat when swimming?

Then it dawned on Libby. Not a hat—clothes perhaps. Clothes bundled tightly and tied on top of the swimmer's head. If he held his head above water, the clothes wouldn't get wet.

Libby felt sure that was the shape she had seen. But there wouldn't have been time for the person to change. If the swimmer really did come on board, where had he gone? He would have been soaking wet.

Still curious, Libby leaned forward for a better look. The wooden crate was a large one and just the right height for someone to sit on. Protected by the overhang of the deck above, it had stayed dry, in spite of the heavy dew of early morning.

Dry except for one place!

On the top of the crate was a clear mark where someone had sat in wet clothing. On the floor in front of the crate the deck was also wet, as though a puddle had formed around the man's feet. And next to the crate, where a wooden slat and the deck met, there was a thin line of water.

Staring at the telltale marks, Libby felt a sudden jolt of fear. *Whoever the man is, I stood right in front of him. In the middle of the night, when everyone else was asleep, I stood here talking to him.*

As she tried to push aside the panic tightening her throat, Libby knew one thing. *I've got to tell Pa right away.*

Taking the stairs two at a time, Libby raced back up to the top of the boat. Pa's cabin was at the front of the texas deck, just ahead of Libby's room.

A moment after she knocked their special code, her tall, slender father opened the door. Except for the touch of white above his ears, Pa's wavy black hair was as dark as his captain's uniform.

Now Pa's smile welcomed her, and Libby felt better just being with him. When she told him what had happened, his face grew serious.

"And what was the guard's name?" he asked.

"Swenson, Pa. He said it was Charlie Swenson."

A puzzled look filled Pa's eyes. "I can't remember any crew

member by that name, but I'll check. Our first mate could have hired someone in St. Paul or Stillwater."

Pa followed Libby down to the main deck. When she showed him the faint outline of damp wood, he nodded. "Good for you, Libby. Someone in wet clothes sat here, all right. The night air was so damp it didn't dry as fast as it would in a wind."

When Pa sought out the first mate, Libby went with him.

"Any crew by the name of Charlie Swenson?" Captain Norstad asked.

Mr. Bates shook his head. "No, sir. No one by that name. But I have no doubt that a guard was on duty at the time. I kept a close watch last night because of the escaped prisoner."

"Could the guard have left his place by the gangplank for a short time?" Libby asked quickly.

"He made his rounds, circling the main deck every twenty minutes."

"We better change that rule," Captain Norstad said. "The next time we need a guard have him change the amount of time between rounds so that someone watching won't know what to expect. And put on two guards—one on each side of the *Christina*."

As Libby and her father headed for the dining room and breakfast, the captain sighed. "I feel like someone who locked the barn after the horse was stolen. Keep your sharp eyes working, Libby. But come to me at any sign of danger. Taking care of men who creep on board is my job, not yours. All right?"

"All right, Pa." Her father's hug chased away the scared feelings in Libby's heart.

But then Pa said, "I hope that all the man wants is a free ride."

5

The Disappearing Cookies

*W*hat else would the man want? Libby wondered as she followed Pa up the stairway.

Then Libby's heart thudded to a stop. *Maybe it really is the escaped prisoner. Or it could be someone who knows that Jordan is on board. If Jordan gets caught, he'll lose his freedom and the chance to help his family.*

The moment she finished breakfast, Libby started looking for Caleb and Jordan. Before she did anything else, she had to warn them. Besides, she wanted to tell Caleb about the great way she had figured things out. Libby felt proud of herself.

If Caleb and Jordan know how smart I am, they'll trust me more. They'll let me help with the Underground Railroad. Once before Caleb had allowed her to do something, but that was because he had no choice.

Libby found Caleb and Jordan sitting on the hurricane deck watching a huge log raft being towed down Lake St. Croix. The raft was made up of eight to ten strings of logs fastened side by side. Each of the strings measured about sixteen feet across and four hundred feet long. Around the outer edge were logs joined by chains to hold each raft together.

With the steamboat at the front, strong ropes stretched back to pull the raft along. The men that Caleb called Red Shirts stood on the two ends of the raft. Each of them held the great long pole they used as an oar.

Another man sat on a crate, peeling potatoes. Beyond him were three small buildings. "For the trip down the river each man builds his own little house," Caleb explained. "See how the door is just big enough for a man to crawl in and out?"

Each "house" was only a few boards high, barely giving enough room for one man to lie down. Work pants and red shirts hung over the peaked roof of two of the houses.

Seeing the wet clothing, Libby shivered. Working in the river during this second week of May had to feel like taking a bath in ice water. It reminded her of the reason she had come—to tell Caleb and Jordan about the man who swam out to the *Christina*.

Libby began by telling how she heard a muffled splash during the night. Partway through her story, Jordan started nervously cracking his knuckles. Watching him, all of Libby's proud feelings crumbled. No longer did she want to prove what a great thing she had done in figuring things out.

By the time Libby finished talking, worry filled Jordan's eyes. "Who be this man?" he asked.

"I don't know," Libby answered.

Caleb also looked upset. "And your pa doesn't have any idea?"

Libby shook her head. "He could be the prisoner. He could be almost anyone. It was too dark to see his face."

"Would you recognize his voice?" No longer was Caleb the thirteen-year-old boy who liked to tease Libby. In that one moment he had changed into the Underground Railroad person who was always on guard. As a conductor for the Underground Railroad, Caleb guided runaway slaves from one place of safety to the next.

"His voice?" Libby remembered a slight rasp when the man spoke, but that could mean he had a cold. *Or swam in cold water*.

"His voice had a strange rasp—almost like he was hoarse," she said.

As though needing to tell himself the man wasn't someone who would spoil the rescue of his family, Jordan began talking. "When I was just a little boy Momma told me, 'Jordan, your daddy and I, we name you for what you is goin' to do.'

" 'What you mean, Momma?' I wanted to know.

" 'You is goin' to lead our people out of slavery,' Momma said. 'You is goin' to lead our people to the Promised Land.' "

Long ago Libby had learned about Moses leading the Israelites out of slavery in Egypt. Forty years later, Joshua brought them across the Jordan River into Canaan, the Promised Land.

"Over and over Momma told me till she didn't need to tell me no more," Jordan went on. "I knew for myself that what Momma said would be true. I been tellin' myself I is goin' to rescue my people. But now I is scared, Caleb. Real scared."

For the first time the difficulty of what Jordan planned seemed to overwhelm him. "I is so scared that I has a hard time believin' I can do what I needs to do."

"Not many fugitives go back to the state where they've been slaves," Caleb warned. "At least your mother lives in a different place from where you were. Her master doesn't know you."

Jordan's troubled gaze met Caleb's. "But can I do what I needs to do? Can I rescue my people?"

For a long moment Caleb did not answer, as if he knew the seriousness of whatever he said. At last he spoke. "When Libby's pa wants to make sure I'm not just rushing off on my own, he looks me straight in the eye. He asks, 'What is God telling you to do?' "

Jordan's gaze fell away. Stretching out his fingers, he stared at his right hand, then his left. Slowly he turned them over to stare at the palms. Then he studied his feet.

"In the Good Book, Moses be a big man," Jordan said, still looking at his feet. "He take his people out of Egypt."

"Out of suffering," Caleb answered quietly.

"Out of slavery." Jordan's voice was still thoughtful.

"These hands—these feet," he said slowly. "Long time ago the Lord told me, 'Jordan, I gives you strong hands—strong feet. I gives them to you so you kin lead your people out of slavery. But I gives you something else—something you is goin' to need even more.' "

When Jordan lifted his head, tears shone in his dark eyes. "The Lord, he told me, 'Jordan, I gives you a big heart—a big enough heart to lead your people to freedom.' "

As though embarrassed by his tears, Jordan tried to wipe them away. But tears filled his eyes again and ran down his cheeks.

When Caleb leaned forward, his gaze never left Jordan's face.

"Your heart *is* big enough to bring your people to freedom," he said. "The freedom of your people means more to you than your life. It might cost you your life."

In the silence Libby heard only the slap of the paddle wheels against water. Then a long steady look passed between Caleb and Jordan.

"If you want me, I'm still planning to help you." Caleb held out his hand, renewing the promise he had made a few weeks before.

This time Jordan did not hesitate. Halfway between the boys, their two hands met.

Then Caleb stood up. "C'mon. I want to show you something."

He led Jordan and Libby to Captain Norstad's cabin. There Caleb opened the large Bible owned by Libby's father. As he turned the pages, Caleb explained.

"A man named Paul was facing some hard things. God told him, 'My grace is enough for you. When you're weak, that's when my power can really help you.'"

As always, Libby felt surprised by the way Caleb could explain things. From the moment she met him, Libby had known there was something different about Caleb. When she discovered what he did with the Underground Railroad, she thought it was that. But soon she learned there was another reason for Caleb being strong.

"The hard things Paul faced helped him learn about God's power," Caleb said. "Paul said, 'When I am weak, then am I strong.'"

In the time since Jordan came on board Caleb had been teaching him to read. Now Caleb pointed to each word. Jordan stared at them as if trying to match the words with what he heard.

"I is weak, all right," he said. "I is mighty scared. And God's grace is enough for me?"

Caleb nodded.

"Long time ago I learned that word," Jordan answered. "Grace be the Lord's love and favor, even though I ain't deservin' of it."

As though forgetting his worries, Jordan straightened, standing tall in the proud look that reminded Libby of royalty. "Our colored preacher told me I is not a slave. I is created in God's image. I is His child!"

Once more Jordan looked down at the pages of the Bible. "All my life I been wantin' to read the Good Book. I been wantin' to see all them good promises for myself. Show me again."

This time it was Jordan who pointed to each word, repeating what Caleb told him. Soon Jordan said, "Stand back! I is reading to *you*."

Pointing to each word, Jordan read the promise. " 'When I am weak, then am I strong.' "

As though wanting to prove that he understood what he read, Jordan lifted his head and faced Caleb. "When I is weak, Jesus makes me strong!"

At Prescott, Wisconsin, where the waters of the St. Croix flowed into those of the Mississippi River, the towboat dropped its lines. From there to Pepin, where the river again widened into a lake, the lumber raft would drift on the current, guided by the oars of the Red Shirts.

As the *Christina* drew near the landing at Prescott, Libby spoke quickly. "I want to help too," she told Jordan. "I want to help you rescue your family."

For a long moment Jordan sat quietly, thinking about it. When he spoke, his voice was low but sure. "There be all kinds of people workin' with the Underground Railroad. Free blacks, white men and women, boys and girls. But I ain't never heard of no white girl tryin' something that hard. To go into Missouri—"

Jordan shook his head. "Not unless there be a mighty big reason. But I thanks you for wanting to try."

Listening to Jordan's quiet voice, Libby knew his mind was made up. Even so, she didn't want to accept his words. *If I try really hard—if I do everything perfect, I'll convince both Caleb and Jordan that I can help bring his family to freedom.*

Three-story warehouses stood along the waterfront at Prescott. Before continuing up the Mississippi River to St. Paul, large steamboats often unloaded their freight there for storage. Then smaller steamboats took the freight on to Stillwater and other towns along the St. Croix River.

When Libby went into the large general store at Prescott, she found it filled with the men who came off the rafts to buy supplies. All of them wore the red shirts that would help someone rescue them if they fell into the water.

Seeing the crowd of men, Libby started to back out. Then the storekeeper asked, "How can I help you?"

While living in Chicago, Libby had taken drawing lessons from a well-known artist. Already Libby had used up the drawing paper she had bought in St. Louis. Now she was glad to find more paper, and pencils as well.

As she paid her money, she noticed a man near a table filled with red shirts. Dressed in gray pants, white shirt, red and blue jacket, and a cap, he seemed out of place—too well dressed compared with all the rafting men who crowded the store. Yet to Libby's surprise he picked up a red shirt.

While the storekeeper wrapped Libby's package, she looked around. If the store carried any other color of shirt, it was nowhere in sight.

Soon the man in the red and blue jacket stepped into line behind six or seven men waiting to pay for their purchases. As Libby watched, the man glanced around as if checking to see who stood behind him.

The artist part of Libby wondered about his quick, almost secret glance. During art lessons, she had learned to notice how a person looked. *If I were going to draw that man, what would I do?* Curious now, Libby moved over next to the door and stood there as if waiting for someone.

The man was about six feet tall and strongly built. For some reason he seemed familiar.

But who do I know in this area? Libby wondered. In Stillwater she had met Nate and the farmer who helped them after the accident. For just a moment she had talked with a few other people. None of them fit this man's description. *Maybe I'm jumpy because of the escaped prisoner*, Libby thought.

Reaching the counter, the man put down his money. When the store owner gave him change, the man turned just enough to find Libby staring at him. As their gaze met, he lifted his hand, touched the visor on his cap, and politely nodded. Then, taking his time, he left the store.

When Libby followed him outside, she watched to see if he would board the *Christina*. Instead, he headed for a different steamboat, a small one of the kind that operated on the St. Croix River. Libby watched until the man started up the gangplank.

All the way back to the *Christina*, Libby thought about it, comparing the escaped prisoner to the man she had just seen. When the prisoner went over the fence, he had a half-shaved head. The hair he had left was light brown, but Libby could not see the color of his eyes. This man wore a cap that sat low on his head. From beneath the visor, a strand of light brown hair hung down over his forehead. His eyes were blue.

The whole thing bothered Libby, and she didn't understand why. Then, as she started up the gangplank, she thought she knew. In Stillwater it had taken only one look to know that the prisoner was doing something wrong. But the man in the store seemed just the opposite. He had met Libby's gaze as though he had no guilty conscience. Only one thing had caused her to look twice—that quick glance over his shoulder.

Maybe I imagined it, Libby thought. *He seems to have nothing to hide.*

Even so, she felt uneasy about the man. *What should I remember?* she asked herself. *My feeling that something was wrong? Or his acting as though everything was all right?*

When Libby reached the gangplank she found roustabouts—men who loaded and unloaded the boat—carrying heavy sacks of grain onto the *Christina*. As Libby's stomach growled with hunger, she realized it was still a long time until lunch. Taller than most girls her age, Libby sometimes wondered if she needed extra food just to fill her up. She only knew there was nothing wrong with her appetite.

Libby decided to find Caleb's grandmother. When Libby first came on board, she called her *Granny*. More and more, Libby thought of her as *Gran*, the way Caleb did.

As head pastry cook, Gran worked in the galley just in front of one of the large paddle wheels. Her gray-white hair was pulled back and twisted into a knot at the top of her head. Smile wrinkles surrounded eyes that made her seem young.

As always, Gran's kitchen was spotless. As usual, she took one look at Samson and said, "You can't come into my kitchen."

Samson looked up with his great brown eyes as though begging for food. Just the same, he seemed to know Gran was boss. Flopping down on his stomach, he lay as close to the door as he could get without crossing the threshold.

The kitchen smelled warm and good with the scent of baking cookies. As Gran took a pan out of the oven, Samson watched every move she made. With his long tongue hanging out, he waited.

"Want to help?" Gran asked Libby as she often did. When Gran turned a pan over to her, Libby shifted the cookies onto a cooling rack.

Working quickly, Gran slipped yet another pan into the oven. This time of the year the *Christina* often carried three hundred people, counting both passengers and crew. Feeding all of them three times a day kept Gran and her helpers busy.

As soon as the cookies were cool enough, Gran filled a plate. "Why don't you share them with Caleb and Jordan," she suggested.

Libby found the boys near the gangplank watching the roustabouts. Over the winter, farmers had filled the Prescott warehouses with wheat to be shipped by boat to the railroad at Dunleith, Illinois.

"Present from Gran," Libby said as she set down the plate on a crate where Caleb sat.

The oatmeal cookies were larger than most cookies. Libby eyed the plate. There were three for each of them, and one person would get four. She wouldn't mind if she were that person.

I should have sneaked a cookie coming here, she thought. Picking up one of them, she bit into it. "Mmmm," she said. "Gran's the best cook in the whole world."

The cookie was still warm in the middle and Libby felt sure she had never tasted anything better. "Help yourself, Jordan," she offered.

As he took a cookie, one of the deckhands spoke to Caleb. For a moment Caleb listened, then told Libby, "Be right back."

When he returned five minutes later, Caleb said, "Now I'll have one of those great cookies."

But when Libby reached for the plate, it was empty!

6

Rope Tricks

"Hey, Libby, what did you do—eat the whole plateful?" Caleb asked.

Libby stared at him. "I only had one cookie."

Caleb held up the empty plate. "How can such a skinny girl have such a good appetite? We have to think of a good name for you. How about something having to do with your red hair?"

That made Libby even more upset. In her Chicago school the boys had a hundred nicknames for her red hair. She was going to stop this nonsense right now.

As though she loved her red hair more than anything in the world, Libby pulled forward a long strand. Here on deck the sunlight brought out the gold highlights.

"I do have nice hair, don't I?" she asked, as if Caleb had given a compliment. "But I did *not* eat more than one cookie. You slipped those cookies off the plate when I wasn't looking."

"Me? I didn't have one," Caleb insisted.

"It's okay if you ate them all," Libby said. "Just be honest about it."

"I am," Caleb answered. "I did not eat one cookie. Ask Jordan. He'll tell you."

"Oh, I get it." Libby was growing frustrated. "Jordan, *you* ate all of them behind my back."

But Jordan shook his head. According to him, he too had eaten only one cookie.

Libby looked from one to the other. "You're teasing me," she said. "You're just pretending you don't know where the cookies are."

"We didn't take them," Caleb insisted. His blue eyes looked as innocent as a baby's.

Suddenly Libby giggled. "Now if Samson were here—" Libby turned to see the great black dog crossing the deck toward them. "He'd swallow a plateful of cookies in one big chomp!"

Libby stared at him. The dog had no crumbs on his muzzle. "Samson, you didn't!" Still, his long tongue reached out as though licking his chops. "Maybe you did!"

Instead of going to Libby, Samson surprised her by edging close to Jordan. On the way upstream the two had gotten to know each other. It looked as though the dog was still protecting Jordan. After the tall boy petted him, Samson walked over to Libby.

As soon as the sacks of wheat were loaded, the *Christina* put out into the Mississippi River for the trip to Dunleith, Illinois. Below Red Wing the river again widened, this time into Lake Pepin. Here too, Libby saw a towboat pulling a log raft. According to Caleb the tow would leave the raft at Read's Landing. From there the raft would again drift on the current to Winona, Minnesota, or La-Crosse, Wisconsin, Clinton or LeClaire, Iowa, or as far away as Hannibal or St. Louis, Missouri.

During the evening meal, Captain Norstad spoke to Libby in a low voice. "One of the passengers is missing his pocket watch."

"Are you wondering what I'm wondering?" she asked. The man who boarded the *Christina* at Stillwater had never been far from her thoughts.

"The passenger said that the chain holding the watch had a loose link. Maybe the chain gave way. The man could have lost the watch when he got off the boat at Prescott." But when Pa's honest eyes met Libby's, she knew he was trying to talk himself into something he didn't really believe.

When supper was over Libby followed Pa up to his cabin. There she told him about the man she had noticed in the Prescott store. "I saw him start up the gangplank of another steamboat," she said.

Now Libby realized she should have been more careful. The man could have started up, but also might have come back down and boarded the *Christina* instead.

"If the man wore the red shirt now, he'd be easy to spot," Pa answered. "Going downriver all the loggers ride the rafts. But when we come back up, we have all kinds of Red Shirts on board. They need the ride to the St. Croix River."

Hoping to learn if the man was on board, Pa and Libby walked through the *Christina.* When they found no one who resembled the escaped prisoner or the man Libby had seen at Prescott, she felt relieved. But then Libby remembered. Anyone who wanted to stay out of sight could just hide behind large pieces of freight or slip into another part of the boat.

In the end, Libby wondered if their search had been a waste of time. Though Pa didn't say it, he looked as if he felt the same way.

"Do you know what bothers me?" Libby said finally. "If the man who climbed on board at Stillwater is still here, he seems mighty clever. And dangerous too."

Even so, Libby felt strangely comforted just from talking to Pa. *It helps telling him what bothers me*, she thought. *Nothing feels quite as scary.*

Always Libby felt proud of her father, and this was one of those moments. When she looked up into his dark brown eyes, she saw Pa's love for her. It reminded Libby of his promise before she came to live on the *Christina.* *"I want a never-give-up family,"* she had told him. *"A family that sticks together, even when it's hard."*

"That's the kind of family I want too," Pa had answered. *"We can be that family for each other."*

"With just two people?"

Pa nodded. *"If we don't give up on each other."*

Now Libby slipped her hand inside Pa's. "I like being part of a never-give-up family," she said softly.

"More trouble," Pa said to Libby the next morning. The *Christina* had tied up at Dunleith, across the river from Dubuque, Iowa, to transfer the heavy sacks of wheat to railroad cars. When the *Christina* again headed downstream, Pa took Libby along when he talked with Caleb.

"A passenger is missing a coat and hat," Pa told them. "That's not something he could drop or lose like a watch. Either the escaped prisoner is on board or we have another thief."

"What do the hat and coat look like?" Libby asked.

"The coat is long and black. The hat is black felt."

"That's exactly what most of the first-class men on this boat are wearing!"

"I know." Pa sighed. "And I'm sure the thief knows it too. But there's something I want the two of you to do. I believe the thief is entering the first-class cabins while the passengers are eating. My officers and I need to be at our table as we usually are. If we aren't there, the thief probably won't try anything."

"We'll keep watch during meals," Caleb said quickly.

"But every cabin has two doors," Libby said. "The thief could use either door."

On the boiler deck where first-class passengers had their rooms, one door opened onto the deck around the outside of the *Christina*. The other door opened to the large main cabin where meals were served. This huge room stretched from one end of the boat to the other with the passenger rooms along the sides.

Captain Norstad asked Libby and Caleb to keep watch on one side of the boat. "I'll get someone else for the other half," he said. "Stay together and keep moving."

They made a quick stop at Galena to pick up bars of lead for the St. Louis market. Soon after the *Christina* continued down the river, the bells signaled mealtime. As passengers left their rooms for the main cabin, Libby and Caleb started walking. Quickly they passed along the outer deck, through the dark hallway behind the large paddle wheel, and back along the deck again. When they reached the double doors at the forward end of the boat, they looked into the dining room. Along the walls were the inside doors to the passenger rooms.

Except for the serving people, everyone was seated. Those who served the food all wore white coats. If anyone else stood up, Libby and Caleb would be able to spot that person at once.

"That makes our job easier," Caleb said. Turning around, he started back the way they had come. Without speaking, Libby followed behind.

"What's the matter?" Caleb asked as they reached the paddle wheel again.

When Libby did not answer, Caleb tried to look into her eyes. But Libby glanced away.

"Are you still mad about the cookies?" Caleb asked. "I can get more from Gran."

What a silly thing to be mad about, Libby thought suddenly. She looked up, ready to make peace with Caleb. But just beyond him, in the area where passengers walked for exercise, she saw a newspaper blowing about on the deck. Running toward it, Libby snatched up the pages.

When Libby saw a headline on the first piece of paper, she gasped. Darting here and there, she snatched up the other pages before they blew overboard. When she had them all, she started arranging them by page number.

"You're forgetting what your pa said," Caleb told her. "We're supposed to be watching for a thief."

"You watch," Libby said. "It's the Stillwater paper! Someone must have brought it on board at one of our stops."

The minute Libby had the pages in order she looked back down the long corridor outside the passenger rooms. "No one there. It's safe," she said.

Returning to the first page, Libby checked the date. "It's the paper that came out yesterday, right after we left!"

"C'mon, we need to keep walking." But now Caleb was interested too.

Then Libby found it—the article she had dreaded. "Right on the front page," she said. "Right there where everyone will see."

As she started reading, Caleb looked over her shoulder.

ANOTHER ACCIDENT ON STILLWATER HILL

Though not on Nelson's Grade, site of another accident, this week's near tragedy points to a growing problem—our need for railings on steep hills.

The article went on to tell what happened, but Libby barely read the description. Instead, her eye jumped ahead to the name *Jordan Parker*.

"There!" Libby pointed. "See what the paper calls him? A cabin boy on the *Christina*. And there. It tells about Jordan's accident on the way to St. Paul."

Caleb took the newspaper from her.

"You said you didn't tell the reporter about Jordan!" Libby exclaimed.

"I didn't," Caleb answered calmly.

"But there it is! Right there." Libby nearly poked a hole through the paper. "How could you, Caleb? With all you've done to protect Jordan, how could you do this now?"

"I didn't," Caleb said again.

"Then who did?"

Caleb thought about it. "Nate could have said something, but we didn't tell him what happened to Jordan on the way to St. Paul."

Somehow that upset Libby even more. "I know," she said. "A reporter is like a detective. He gets some information from one person, and more information from someone else. Then he puts all the pieces together."

"Oh, Libby, calm down," Caleb said.

Instead, Libby's voice rose in anger. "You gave Jordan away! You got his name put in the paper when he's a runaway slave!"

"It doesn't say anything about Jordan being a fugitive."

"But someone might stop him from bringing his family out of slavery! Someone might fit it all together, just like the reporter fit pieces together. Jordan has a big reward on his head!"

"Shhh!" Caleb warned. "You'll be the one to give Jordan away."

Suddenly Libby looked up. Beyond Caleb, near the corner of the wall behind him, something moved.

Not something, Libby thought. *Someone.*

Instantly she took off, racing down the deck after the person. In the dark hallway between the paddle wheel and the passenger rooms, the person disappeared.

When Libby reached the nearest room, she pounded on the door, but no one answered.

Libby pounded again. "Do I have the right one?" she asked as Caleb caught up.

Just then the door opened. A little old lady peered out. "Yes?" she asked, her voice quivering with fright.

"I'm sorry," Libby said quickly. "I'm mixed up."

Racing along the corridor, she raised her hand, ready to knock at the next door.

Angry now, Caleb stopped her. "Libby, you can't do that."

"Why not?"

"You'll scare every real passenger on your pa's boat. And the thief you want to catch won't answer." Taking her hand, Caleb dragged Libby away.

When they reached the front of the boiler deck it was still empty. Caleb led Libby over to the railing. There he stopped.

"I want to tell you something." Caleb's voice was cold with fury. "We have just missed catching the thief your pa wanted us to find. That was probably him looking for something more to steal."

Standing there, Libby felt her throat tighten. Though she didn't want to admit it, she knew Caleb was right.

"What's more, I did not give Jordan away. I did not give his name, and the reporter said nothing about Jordan being a fugitive."

Again Libby knew Caleb was right. She turned away, unable to bear Caleb's angry eyes. But he wasn't through.

"Except for those people we trust, not one person knew that Jordan isn't a free black. No one knew that he's a fugitive—that there's a reward offered for him. But you talked so loud that anyone who wanted to listen could hear. If the man who heard you is already a thief, it won't be hard for him to figure out what to do."

From deep within, sobs rose in Libby's throat. She wanted to cry out, telling Caleb how sorry she was. But when she turned back to him, only angry words spilled out. "Caleb Whitney, I don't care what you think!"

"I'm going now," he answered, his voice still cold with anger. "I'm looking for your father's thief, though I'm sure I won't find him."

Without speaking, Libby followed Caleb around the boiler deck. Yet she knew it would do no good. Even worse, Caleb would not even glance her way.

When at last the two servings of dinner were finished, Libby clutched the newspaper to herself and hurried to the stairs. By the time she reached her room on the texas deck, tears blinded her eyes. *Caleb hates me*, she thought. But that wasn't the worst. Libby now hated herself.

How could I talk so loud about such an important secret? Libby moaned to herself. With all her heart she wanted Jordan to stay free. With all her heart she wanted to help Jordan's family. Instead, with a few angry words she had ruined everything.

My dream, Libby thought. Now she knew that's what it was. *My dream was to help Jordan's family and other families like his.* Now that dream was gone, like water dashing against the rocks, then falling away.

Caleb will never trust me again. And Jordan—when Jordan finds out, he'll hate me for what I did to him.

Again Libby started crying. She was still sobbing when she fell asleep.

When Libby woke up, she had no idea what time it was. She knew only that it must be the middle of the night. For a moment she lay there, wondering what had brought her out of a sound sleep. Her head hurt. Her eyes felt swollen. She wondered what had gone wrong.

Then she remembered. *Someone heard me give away Jordan's secret. Someone we probably can't trust. Whoever that man is, he now knows that Jordan is a fugitive!*

In her misery Libby cried out to God. "I told you I loved you. I asked for your forgiveness. How can you let this happen to me?!"

Her anger growing, Libby pounded her fists against the mattress. *I thought that when I became a Christian, life would be easier. That I would say and do all the right things. I wanted to do something good—to help Jordan's family. Instead, I've wrecked* everything!

Just then Libby's stomach rumbled. *And I'm hungry besides!*

Visions of food started to dance in Libby's head. *An apple. Where can I get an apple?* Libby didn't know. Then she remembered Gran's big oatmeal cookies. Gran had showed her where they were in case Libby ever got hungry.

When Libby's feet touched the floor, she realized that she had fallen asleep still wearing her dress. Only then did Libby remember. The night before she had been so upset that for the first time in her life she had not eaten supper.

This time Libby felt afraid to walk around the boat without Samson along. When she opened the door on the side of the deck where Samson slept, the great black Newfoundland stood up. As though sensing how Libby felt, he came close, brushing against her.

Following just behind Libby's heels, Samson stayed with her all the way down to Gran's kitchen. There Libby found six giant cookies—three for herself and three for Samson.

Taking the cookies along, Libby walked back to the front of the boat. At the top of the wide steps, she sat down in the shadows. Again Samson edged close, as though making sure Libby was all right. Flopping onto the step beside her, he stretched out. Each time Libby gobbled a cookie, she slipped one to Samson.

From here Libby looked down over the bow of the *Christina*. As her eyes grew used to the night, she stared ahead at the dark water and even darker trees along the shore. A stiff wind had kicked up, and the cool night air felt good after the warmth of the day.

Near the place where the gangplank usually went out, a lantern hung from a post, offering dim light. On the forward deck, crew and deck passengers lay on crates, barrels, and piles of wood— whatever they could find for a place to sleep.

As the flag whipped in the wind, Libby thought about Jordan's plans to rescue his family. It was hard to believe that in only a few hours he and Caleb would leave the boat. But Libby didn't even know where. *Burlington, Iowa? Keokuk, Iowa? Where will they get off?*

Coming upriver, Caleb had stopped in both towns. Yet, during all the times and ways he and Jordan made plans, they had never talked in front of her.

They didn't take a chance, Libby thought, feeling angry at herself again. *Maybe Caleb knew I couldn't keep a secret.*

Now there was one thing Libby felt sure about. They would leave without her. She no longer had even one tiny bit of hope that she could go along.

By the time Libby finished the cookies she felt sleepy. Yawning once, then twice, she decided she better go back to bed. Suddenly a tall shape came around the corner at the bottom of the steps. Quietly he walked across the forward deck to the bow of the boat. For a moment the person stood there, not moving, staring ahead as Libby had.

Then he straightened. Throwing back his shoulders, he reached up. With arms stretched above him, he raised his hands to the sky. Standing tall, he stretched as high as he could reach.

Instantly Libby knew who he was. *Jordan.*

The first night he came on board Jordan had raised his arms, as though celebrating his freedom. Was he thinking about what it meant to stand free under a starlit sky?

As the moment passed, Jordan lowered his arms. Yet he stood there still, as though wanting to feel the cool night air—the air of freedom—against his face.

Just then someone lying on one of the crates raised his head, then sat up. When Jordan turned away from the bow, the person quickly lay down. Yet the dark outline of his body had shifted. The man now lay on his side where he could see Jordan's movements.

Finding his way between the sleeping people, Jordan started back across the deck. Closer and closer he came toward the steps where Libby waited. Behind Jordan, the man on the crate sat up again. Without making a sound, he got to his feet and followed Jordan.

Suddenly the man's arm shot up. A loop of rope whirred through the air. Passing over Jordan's head, it settled around his chest.

Snapping tight, the rope jerked Jordan to a halt. As he struggled to free himself, the man moved toward him, drawing up the end of the rope as he went.

7

Bad News

$\mathcal{F}$illed with terror, Libby leaped to her feet. From deep in his throat Samson growled, "Wooooof!" In the next moment the dog started down the steps.

Just then Jordan's right arm broke free. As the man came up behind him, Jordan thrust his elbow backward. With a quick, sharp movement he jabbed the man in the stomach. A sharp *oooff!* broke the quiet of the night.

With another swift jerk, Jordan pulled the rope from the man's hands. Clutching the rope, Jordan bounded toward the stairs. Taking two steps at a time, he raced past where Libby stood in the shadows.

In panic Libby looked back to the deck. Already the man had disappeared.

As Samson returned to her, Libby breathed deeply with relief. *Jordan is safe—for now.* The whole thing had happened so fast it didn't seem real.

Then there was something about which Libby felt very sure. *That was the man who heard me talking. Whoever he is, he's been watching for a chance to capture Jordan and collect the reward.*

There was no other way to explain the man on the deck. Without doubt Libby knew what a truly awful thing she had done. *This happened to Jordan because of me.*

Dropping down on the step again, Libby buried her head in her lap. Deep inside she felt a big lump as if her feelings had tied into a knot with the awfulness of what she had seen. Nuzzling against her, Samson licked her arm, but Libby paid no attention. *I gave away a secret I needed to keep.*

When she finally lifted her head, Libby knew one thing. *I can't handle this by myself. I've got to talk to someone.*

For a moment she wished it could be Ma. As she pushed aside the lonely ache that came whenever she thought of her mother, Libby remembered Gran. By now she would be up, shaping bread dough into rolls for breakfast. In the wee hours of morning, Libby found Gran in the pastry kitchen.

"What's wrong?" she asked the minute she saw Libby's face.

When Libby dropped down on a chair, her words spilled out. "I told a secret," she said.

"Some secrets aren't meant for keeping," Gran answered. "If someone does something wrong and says you can't tell, for instance. Was it that kind of secret?"

"No, Gran." Libby felt ashamed. "It's the kind of secret that should have been kept."

As Gran filled pan after pan with bread dough, Libby told the story. She started with what happened while she and Caleb were supposed to keep watch. She ended with the man who threw a rope over Jordan.

"It's my fault," Libby said.

Gran sighed. "Much as I hate to say it, I think you're right. Everything fits. It was dark on deck. No one else was watching. No one who objects to slavery saw Jordan being caught. All the man had to do was hide Jordan and take him off the boat when we reach a slave state."

"I'm sorry, Gran," Libby said. "It's a terrible thing to give away such an important secret."

"Yes, it is." Gran was honest about it. "You hurt Jordan and his family, but it's much more. You put a great number of people in danger. Do you understand how the Underground Railroad works?"

"I think so," Libby said.

But Gran went on. "Let's imagine what would happen if a slave catcher saw a fugitive enter a station—a house where people hide runaway slaves. The slave catcher might not pounce there. He could watch and wait till that slave went on to the next station, and the next, and the next. If the fugitive and the people who helped him didn't hide what they were doing, a slave catcher would soon know a whole route. And he'd know the conductors—the people like Caleb who take fugitives from one station to the next."

The idea upset Gran so much that sparks of anger lit her eyes. Wiping the flour from her hands, she dropped down on a chair next to Libby.

"It's secrecy that makes the Underground Railroad work, Libby. I know the people who send runaway slaves to me. I know how to send fugitives to the next person. That's all I *need* to know. Someone like Caleb knows many more people and places. But probably only a few people know the main routes across Iowa."

"You know only what you need to know," Libby said slowly.

"It's better that way," Gran said. "Otherwise, if one person gives something away, there could be a great number of people who get hurt."

Libby felt afraid to tell Gran her dream, yet it spilled out. "I wanted to help Jordan's family. I want to help many runaway slaves. But look what I did!"

No longer did Libby believe she could do anything she set out to do. Instead, she knew how easily she could fail. Because of that, being part of the Underground Railroad seemed even more difficult—even impossible.

Suddenly Libby wished she could take the first train to Chicago. *I want to go back to living with Auntie Vi. I want to be where life is easier, even if it isn't as exciting.*

Gran covered the pans with towels, then sat down again. "You want to run, don't you?" she asked as if she guessed Libby's thoughts. "You want to give up and forget about the whole problem of slavery."

Libby stared at her. "How did you know?"

"Because I've often thought the same thing. It would be much simpler not being involved. I wouldn't have to watch every word

I say. I wouldn't be so afraid for Caleb."

"You're afraid?" Libby asked.

"Often I'm afraid," Gran answered. "Caleb is my only grandson."

"Then why do you let him be part of the Underground Railroad?"

When Gran spoke Libby knew she had often thought about her answer. "For every one of us there comes a time when we make a choice about what we believe," Gran said. "We don't know how it's going to affect our life or the people we love. When I made my choice, I said to myself, 'Slavery for any human being is wrong. I'm going to do what I can to change it.'"

"Was it hard for you—at first, I mean?"

"It's still hard." Gran's smile reached her eyes. "You see, I was involved in the Underground Railroad before Caleb. That's why Caleb got involved. He was only nine years old, but he caught on to what I was doing."

"So your choice became his."

"He chose for himself," Gran explained. "But I don't know if he would have made that choice if I hadn't."

"Strange," Libby said. She thought back to the day when Caleb took her to the slave auction in St. Louis. "I wouldn't have wanted to help if Caleb hadn't opened my eyes."

Gran nodded. She understood that too. "Since I decided to help fugitives, my life has never been the same. I haven't succeeded at everything I've tried. But I haven't lost a passenger."

"That's what I'm talking about." Tears welled up in Libby's eyes again. "I've already failed. I even put Jordan's life in danger."

"Have you told God you're sorry?" Gran asked.

Libby shook her head. "He doesn't like me."

"Oh, Libby!" Gran exclaimed. "Why do you think that?"

Libby found it hard to explain, but when she tried, the words tumbled out. "I thought if I became a Christian that I'd say and do all the right things. Instead—" Libby stopped, unable to go on.

As she began to weep, she turned away from Gran. But Gran's arms surrounded her, holding Libby tight. When she finally stopped crying, Gran's voice was soft.

"There's a secret you need to know, Libby. Just because you're a Christian doesn't mean your life will be easier, or that you'll be perfect. But if you let Him, God will help you with whatever you face."

"Then everything will be okay?"

"Not quite," Gran said. "Sometimes we have to live with what happens because of what we did."

"You mean Jordan and his family might still suffer because of what I did."

Gran nodded. "I'm afraid so."

"And there's nothing I can do to change that?"

"Pray," Gran said. "See if God brings something good out of this. All right?"

Libby found it hard to believe that something good could possibly come from what she had done. But if Gran said so, *maybe* it was true.

When Libby stood up to go, she was no longer afraid to look into Gran's blue eyes. "Thanks," Libby said softly. Her shoulders no longer slumped, and she held her head a bit higher. *Maybe I understand Jordan's proud look just a little better. He's not proud in the wrong way. He just knows how God can help him.*

When Libby stepped out on the deck, the eastern sky was pink. *A new day*, Libby thought. She breathed deeply. The fresh morning air brought comfort to her heart. *Maybe the most important thing about failing is what I learn from it.*

It was too early in the morning to set things right with Caleb and Jordan, but Libby's thoughts leaped ahead. *Okay. So I can't go on the trip. But I'm going to believe that Jordan's family will get here safely. If they do, what will they need?*

When Libby reached the texas deck, she realized that Samson was still trailing her. As he swished his big muzzle in his bowl of water, Libby opened the door of her room. She took one look at her quilts, and knew what to do. Once before she had given them away. Now they were back, washed and clean—ready for someone who might need them more than she did.

Again Libby thought ahead. It might be hard sneaking Jordan's family on board and into the secret hiding place. When they came, they could be wet and cold from walking in rain. What if it was impossible to give them something warm?

This would be a good time, Libby thought. *Most of the passengers are still sleeping. But how can I carry quilts so that no one guesses what I'm doing?*

More than once Caleb had warned Libby that there were Southern sympathizers on board—people who supported the idea of slavery. One of these people was Bates, the first mate. Libby's stomach tightened with dread just thinking about him. But there was an even bigger problem—the man who tried to catch Jordan during the night—and Libby didn't know who he was.

Then Libby remembered that her father had warm wool blankets. It would take two trips to carry her quilts and his blankets. That meant twice as much chance of being seen.

Going out on deck, Libby looked around. As she tried to decide what to do, Samson nudged his empty food bowl. With a quiet *woof* he reminded her that he was hungry.

Suddenly Libby laughed. Newfoundland dogs were known for helping people carry loads. "Don't worry, I'll get you food," she told Samson. "But you'll have to work for it."

Libby told the dog to stay, then raced down the steps. In the engine room she got pieces of rope and flew back up the stairs. Quickly she rolled her quilts as tightly as she could, then tied rope around them. In Pa's cabin she did the same with his blankets.

On his bed she left a note.

> I need your blankets, Pa. Can you buy quilts or blankets for both of us in St. Louis?

Back outside again Libby put her father's blankets on Samson's back. Carefully she balanced the load so it wouldn't be hard for the dog on the stairs. "As soon as we're done, you get to eat," Libby promised.

Down the few steps from the texas to the hurricane deck Libby went, then down the longer flight to the boiler deck. Samson followed her as if he did this every day of his life. On the main deck, Libby walked into the cargo room behind the stairs. Close to the door into the engine room was a small but heavy-looking piece of

machinery. As though to give it more strength, the machine was mounted on a piece of wood.

Libby glanced around. *No one in sight.*

Her fingers awkward with hurry, Libby untied the blankets. Kneeling down, she pushed the wood base under the machine. When it moved to one side, she pulled up the hatch underneath. Quickly she tossed Pa's blankets down the hole. With a thud they landed on the floor of the hull, five feet below.

Just as quickly Libby closed the opening and pulled the machine back in place. As she stood up, she heard footsteps. Libby took her place next to Samson and started walking. A moment later Mr. Bates appeared.

"Good morning, Miss Libby," he said.

"Good day, Mr. Bates," Libby answered.

"Up bright and early, aren't you? Exercising your dog?"

Libby gulped, remembering she should not lie.

"See how he's learning to mind me?" she asked instead. Telling Samson to stay, she walked toward the door that lead to the forward deck. There she turned and called.

Samson came to her at once, and Libby kept walking. In spite of the cool morning she felt warm with nervousness.

Another trip still, she thought, dreading the idea.

Back on the texas deck again, she piled her quilts on the Newfoundland's back. "I'm training you to carry loads, Samson," she said. "If anyone asks, you remember that."

Once again Libby started out. As she passed onto the boiler deck she found first-class passengers coming out of their rooms to take their exercise. More than once someone smiled at her and Samson. Giving a quick wave, Libby smiled back but kept going.

When she reached the main deck again, Libby looked around. Sure enough, Bates stood there as if waiting for her. Instead of turning into the cargo room, Libby started around the corner to the side deck. Wherever there was enough space, she walked, called for Samson to follow, then praised him when he did.

"Good dog. Good boy, Samson. You're learning fast," Libby said, loudly enough for Bates to hear.

For at least fifteen minutes Libby waited for the first mate to leave. Finally she headed for Gran's kitchen to get Samson his food. When he finished eating, Libby returned to the forward deck.

To her disappointment Bates was still there. Whenever she glanced his way, Libby saw him looking toward her. At last he seemed to grow tired of watching her. But when he walked up the steps, he turned around when he reached the boiler deck. Just before passing through the doors into the main cabin, he turned again. This time Libby smiled and waved.

Bates was too dignified to wave back. With his back straight and his shoulders stiff, he marched into the dining room.

The minute he disappeared, Libby hurried into the cargo room. With trembling fingers she untied her quilts. Once more she glanced around, making sure that no one watched. Once more she pushed aside the machine and pulled up the secret hatch.

As she picked up a quilt to throw it down the hole, she heard a door open.

8

Jordan's New Plan

Libby's heart pounded. Whirling around, she stared at the two people standing near the door from the engine room. In the dim light it was hard to see their faces.

Then one of them spoke. "What you doin', Libby?"

Libby sagged with relief. Even her knees felt weak. "You scared me, Jordan. I'm bringing blankets for your family." Though they had never talked about it, Libby felt sure that Jordan knew about the hiding place for runaway slaves.

"I thanks you, Libby," Jordan said.

When Caleb stepped forward, Libby felt angry. "You're following me around now?"

It upset Libby. If Caleb and Jordan found it so easy to figure out what she was doing, what about someone else—someone who shouldn't know?

Libby picked up the quilts, tossed them into the hold, closed the hatch, and swung the machinery back into place. With Samson trailing behind her, she stalked off.

"Wait, Libby," Caleb called.

"What for?" Already Libby had forgotten she was going to set things straight with Caleb and Jordan. Instead of helping her hide the quilts and blankets, the boys had watched and followed her, scaring her besides.

As she reached the door to the deck, Caleb caught up. "We need to talk," he said.

"I need to talk," Libby said. "You need to listen. But this isn't the time."

"Yes, it is," Caleb said. "We're leaving soon."

"To start the rescue?" Libby had both dreaded and looked forward to that moment.

When Caleb took the lead, Libby followed him up to the hurricane deck. It was still quiet there and the three could sit down and talk.

"You first, Libby," Caleb said.

Though it was just what she wanted, it was not the way Libby wanted it. With her heart still pounding, she began to explain. "That man on the deck last night—the one who threw a rope around Jordan—"

"You saw him?" Caleb asked. "We were just going to tell you about him."

"I'm sorry, Caleb," Libby said. "I'm sorry for losing my temper, for saying the wrong things, for talking too loud."

But Libby knew this was much bigger than the argument between the two of them. Caleb wasn't just any boy. Since the age of nine, he had risked his own safety for what he believed about the freedom of slaves. He had built up a reputation as someone other people could trust.

As a lump formed in Libby's throat, she swallowed hard. "I'm sorry, most of all, for betraying a secret."

Fighting against tears, Libby turned to Jordan. "I'm sorry, Jordan, for giving you away. For hurting your chances to rescue your family."

"I forgives you, Libby," Jordan said simply.

"You forgive me?" Libby asked. "Just like that?"

"Yes'm. Just like that."

"But that man who threw the rope around you—it was my fault, Jordan. He must have heard me talk. How can you forgive me?"

"I ain't got no choice," Jordan answered.

I ain't got no choice. Like a spinning wheel the words went round and round in Libby's head. As if she were still standing there, she saw Jordan at the auction where he was sold as a slave. She remembered the names he was called. In the weeks between then and now, she had come to a better understanding of how much those names hurt.

Unable to shake the grief in her heart, Libby remembered another time—when Caleb washed the great open wounds of the whip marks across Jordan's back. That was the day when Jordan told them what his daddy had taught him. *"Jordan, hatin' robs your bones of strength, makes you blind when you needs to fight. If you forgive, you be strong."*

Now Jordan leaned forward, as if wanting to be sure Libby understood. "Long time ago my daddy say, 'It ain't how people treats you on the outside that counts. It's what you is on the inside. You got to be sure that be good, 'cause you can't run away from yourself.'"

Libby stared at him. "I can't run away from myself?"

"Wherever you is, you is the person you is goin' to be with."

Libby thought about it. "I don't have any choice about being with Libby Norstad." It almost struck her funny. "I *have* to be with myself!"

Jordan grinned. "You got it!"

In that moment Libby felt as if a weight had fallen off her shoulders. "Okay," she said. "I can't run away from knowing that I did something wrong." Libby looked from Jordan to Caleb. "But I want to be different. I want God to help me start over again."

As Libby stood up to leave, she noticed a well-dressed man standing along the rail. He seemed to be looking out across the river. But Libby had been so busy talking that she hadn't noticed when the man came on deck.

What did he hear? Libby wondered, feeling frantic again. It wasn't hard to tell that he had been listening.

By the time Libby reached the texas deck she remembered Caleb's words. "We'll be leaving soon," he had said. Like a toothache Libby felt her disappointment that she wouldn't be going along.

Inside her room Libby found the newspaper she had dropped on the floor the night before. Taking the scattered pages, she spread them out on the floor to read.

Once again she saw the article about their accident. Nearby was another article, one Libby had missed.

MAN FLEES STILLWATER PRISON

The well-known and dangerous prisoner known as Sam McGrady escaped the Minnesota Territorial Prison yesterday. Before being captured, he was part of a gang that robbed a number of banks in Minnesota Territory and the state of Iowa. During the last holdup before Sam's imprisonment, a bank teller was seriously hurt.

The outlaw is known for his ability to do rope tricks. It is believed that at some time he worked on a ranch in the West. He has been called light-fingered because of the way he makes whatever he steals disappear.

Sam McGrady was seen climbing over the wall of the prison by Nate Johnson of Stillwater and three friends from the steamboat *Christina*. At that time Sam was wearing gray pants and a white shirt. As Nate and the others tried to report his escape, they were involved in the accident reported elsewhere in this paper.

A logger from the upper St. Croix River remembers seeing a man wearing the gray pants, wool cap, and red and blue jacket that is the usual dress of Stillwater prisoners. The escaped prisoner may have hidden in the cave used to store food for the cook shack. If so, he could have boarded a steamboat and left this area.

Sam McGrady may be armed and is thought to be dangerous.

Libby gasped. *That's the man I saw in the store at Prescott! That's exactly what he was wearing. So he has to be the person who threw the rope around Jordan last night!*

Her heart in her throat, Libby snatched up the newspaper and raced out of the room.

When Libby found Pa in his cabin, he too had bad news. A man had just reported a three-piece suit and a white shirt missing.

Libby frowned. *That well-dressed man who came on deck while I talked*

*to Caleb and Jordan. That man was wearing a three-piece suit. But so are a
lot of other men on board.*

"Let me guess," Libby said. "It's a suit like any first-class passenger would wear."

Pa grinned. "As Jordan would say, 'You got it!' "

"If only I could have caught a better look at the prisoner's face,"
Libby said. More than once she had tried to remember what the
man looked like when he came over the wall. She had been too far
away to see even the color of his eyes.

When Libby showed Pa the newspaper article, he said, "I'm not
surprised. At least we know who we're looking for."

After a search of the *Christina*, Libby found Caleb and Jordan in
the baggage room with each of them sitting on a large trunk. As she
drew near they stopped talking, and Libby felt sure they were making plans.

Libby handed Caleb the newspaper. When she sat down, Caleb
read the article aloud. Jordan looked over his shoulder, as though
hoping he could match Caleb's words with words he had learned
to read.

"Uh-oh!" Caleb exclaimed when he finished. "Maybe I did you
wrong, Libby. I wouldn't be surprised if Sam McGrady picked up
our cookies as he came on board."

"I got the feelin' I know that man already," Jordan said. "And I
sure don't like that rope of his."

"He must be the man I saw in the store at Prescott," Libby said.

"If you're right, you're the only one on board who knows what
he looks like," Caleb told her.

Libby hadn't thought about that. "You mean I'm the only one
who can identify him?"

"Yup," Caleb answered. "And he sure knows who you are with
your red hair."

"My *auburn* hair." As Libby tossed her head, her long hair
swung around her shoulders. But Caleb had something more important in mind.

"We're just making final plans to rescue Jordan's mother."

Libby jumped to her feet. "I'll leave so you can talk." For the
first time she felt glad that Jordan and Caleb would make the trip
without her. At least Jordan would be off the boat, away from Sam

McGrady. "If I don't see you before you go, have a safe trip."

But Jordan stopped her. "Hold on there, Libby. Me and Caleb was talking about something."

Libby looked from one to the other. *Arguing, you mean*, she thought. When she sat down again, Jordan held out a slate.

"Caleb taught me how to write *Burlington*," Jordan said proudly. He erased the name and drew a line that stood for the Mississippi River. Next to that line Jordan put a dot, then a *B* for Burlington.

Farther down the Mississippi, Jordan carefully printed a *K* next to a dot for Keokuk, Iowa. Then he drew a line for the Des Moines River. Inland from Keokuk, he put a third dot, and the letter *C*.

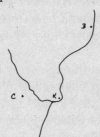

"Cahoka," Jordan said. "In northeast Missouri. That's where Momma is—on a farm in Clark County. Old Massa sold Momma up north from where I was. I ain't never been where Momma and my sisters and my brother are."

Libby waited. Where was this all going to lead? She only knew that on their trip upriver Caleb had gone into Burlington, Iowa. For a while he and Gran had lived there, and Caleb had contacts with the Underground Railroad.

"I talked to some people I know in Burlington." Caleb's voice sounded stiff, as if he really didn't want to tell Libby what was going on. "I asked them to have a peddler's wagon in Keokuk when we came back down the river."

But now Caleb and Jordan agreed that the risk was too great. Sam McGrady would find it a simple matter to follow the high square sides of a peddler's wagon.

"I got a new plan," Jordan told Libby. "Me and Caleb needs to get off in Burlington."

"We'll get horses to ride," Caleb said. "If someone tries to follow us, it won't be as hard to get away from him. We'll travel on land while the *Christina* goes down the river."

Caleb spoke quickly now, and Libby knew they were running out of time. "On the other side of the Des Moines River, we'll get a farm wagon and look like anybody traveling through."

But there Jordan disagreed. "I has to be your driver," he said to Caleb. "You has to be my owner."

A quick flash of something Libby didn't understand crossed Caleb's face. But when he spoke, she heard the grieving in his voice.

"I don't want to even play the part," Caleb said.

"If someone thinks we is friends, you be in big trouble," Jordan answered. "And I be unable to rescue my family."

A long look passed between them. Finally Caleb nodded.

"But you can't look proud," he warned. "If you look proud, anyone who sees you will know it's you. That's how the reward poster described you."

As if he had thought through every detail of his plan, Jordan grinned. "I ain't goin' to look proud. You'll see."

"So, what am I supposed to do?" Libby asked.

As Jordan's gaze met Caleb's, Libby again felt sure there had been a disagreement. But she also knew something else. A few weeks before, Caleb had made a surprising offer to Jordan. *"You tell me what to do, and I'll do it."*

Jordan had leaped up, his eyes blazing with anger. *"You is foolin' me, sure enough! There ain't no slave boy who tells a white boy what to do!"*

But Caleb hadn't been making fun of Jordan. *"I know what to do if I find a runaway slave,"* Caleb had said. *"I know how to hide a fugitive who comes near the Christina. What you need to do will be a whole lot harder."*

From then on, whenever Libby asked if she could help in the rescue, Caleb had followed one rule. It was Jordan planning the trip. Though Libby felt sure that Caleb didn't want her along, he had no choice but to stick to his own words.

Now Libby repeated her question. "What do you want me to do?"

"I wants you to go in that peddler wagon," Jordan said. "I wants you and the peddler to drive right up to that farmhouse. While you does that, me and Caleb sneaks into that farm any way we can. We finds Momma and tells her we is leavin' for the Promised Land."

"You want *me* to talk to the owners?" The memory of how she had failed still haunted Libby. "What if I do the wrong thing?"

"Just because you done one thing wrong don't mean you is goin' to do everything wrong," Jordan told her. "The Lord told me we is goin' to need you."

"*You* need *me*?" Libby looked from one boy to the other. When Caleb did not meet her eyes, Libby knew she had been right. Caleb still did not want her along.

"Why do you want two wagons?" Libby asked.

"If something happens so me and Caleb don't git there, Momma's got another way to escape."

As though he could no longer sit still, Jordan started pacing up and down in the open space between baggage. "It be early mornin' now. We has a whole day to git to the farm and find my family. We needs to rescue them by midnight tonight. If we gits away by then, we has till first light tomorrow mornin' to find a hiding place."

Suddenly Jordan stopped his pacing. "I is feeling more and more uneasy about my family."

"What's wrong?" Caleb asked.

"Right here." Jordan thumped his chest. "I been feeling the jiggles for three, four days now. Something is goin' on with Momma and my sisters and my brother."

"Something bad?" Libby asked.

Jordan nodded. "Something real bad."

"How do you know?"

"I hears it like a warnin' bell. Like the Lord is deep inside me sayin', 'Jordan, you got to git there soon. You got to git there as fast as you can.'"

"Do you understand what's wrong?" Caleb asked as if he had no doubt about Jordan hearing from God.

Jordan shook his head. "But I knows one thing." His face filled with despair. "If my family gits sold away before I git there, I ain't never goin' to see them again."

9

The Red Shirts

"We got to pray," Jordan said. Between two big trunks he dropped down on his knees. "We got to pray right now."

As Jordan stretched his arms high above his head, Libby felt glad there was no one around to see. But then Jordan started praying with the boldness of talking to a good friend. Libby closed her eyes.

"Mighty Jesus, we needs your help. We needs your love and protection and favor. We needs you to blind the eyes and shut the ears of them people who want to hurt us. Open the eyes and open the ears of them people you want to help us."

As though in answer to Jordan's prayer, Libby's eyes flew open. Jordan's eyes were open too. Rocking on his knees, he swayed forward and back, looking up to heaven. "Bring my momma and my brother Zack, my sister Serena, and my little sister Rose safe into your Promised Land!"

As though the Lord had already rescued his family, Jordan sank back on his heels. "Jesus, we thanks you that when we is weak, you makes us strong. Hallelujah! A-men!"

As Caleb looked up, Jordan's gaze met his. Instead of worry, a glad light shone in Jordan's eyes.

I wish I could be so sure of what God can do, Libby thought.

Before long, Jordan left them to get ready for the trip. Libby stayed where she was, leaning against a large piece of baggage. Her head bowed, she felt as if she could barely speak.

I thought I could do whatever I set out to do. Jordan knows more about rescuing his family than any of us. And he knows he can't do it without God. Libby's cheeks burned with shame just remembering how sure of herself she had been.

She still felt uncomfortable with Caleb. Because she knew he didn't want her along, there was something stiff and awkward between them. Now a nagging thought entered Libby's mind. *Caleb doesn't think I can do it. Maybe he's right.*

Yet there was a question Libby needed to ask. "Did you mean it when you told Jordan he could lose his life?"

"I meant it," Caleb answered as though he had no doubt about his words.

"But for Pa—if he got caught with a fugitive, it would be fines or imprisonment. Maybe losing the *Christina*."

Caleb nodded. "He's taking a risk for something he believes in. A risk he wouldn't have to take."

"And for Jordan—" Libby's voice trailed off. "It could be his *life*?"

"He's a fugitive," Caleb reminded.

"But our founding fathers fought for life," Libby said. "That's exactly what the men who signed the Declaration of Independence wanted."

More than once during their history lessons, Pa had talked about the document these men had signed. Now, as though it could give Jordan safety, Libby repeated their words. " 'We hold these truths to be self-evident, that all men are created equal—' "

Caleb joined her. " 'That they are endowed by their Creator with certain unalienable Rights—' "

" 'That among these are Life—' " Libby stopped, unable to go on. This last week life had become very precious to her.

"Are there many runaway slaves who go back for their families?" Libby asked when at last she spoke.

"It's unusual. Sometimes a man escapes and works hard to buy the freedom of his wife and children. But now, since that 1850 fugitive slave law, slave catchers have been chasing fugitives all the way to Canada. It's mighty hard for a fugitive to go back."

"Caleb, how do you know if it's really God talking to Jordan?"

"I watch to see what happens," Caleb said. "I want to know if it's something good, like God's protection. If Jordan is hearing the Lord, it should help people, not hurt them."

"So it turns out that Jordan has done the best thing?" Libby asked

Caleb nodded, but Libby still felt scared. She remembered Jordan's owner, the cruel slave trader. "Is Jordan going to have trouble with Riggs again?"

To Libby's surprise Caleb started pacing the floor in much the same way Jordan had. That worried Libby even more. Usually Caleb stayed calm even when really awful things happened. Now he was clearly nervous about what Jordan planned to do.

"Riggs is a really big slave trader, Libby. He's a rich man with lots of property. I'm surprised he's chased Jordan as much as he has. He hasn't got time to run around after one slave, unless—"

A dark, angry look came into Caleb's eyes.

"Unless what?" Though Libby wanted to know, she dreaded the answer.

Caleb stopped pacing. "Remember how Riggs said, 'I never had a slave get away from me—alive, that is!' Riggs might have a special hatred for Jordan because he *did* get away. If it becomes a matter of revenge—"

"Riggs could chase Jordan to the end of the earth," Libby said slowly, disliking even the sound of her words. "You mean Riggs might want to prove to himself that no one can get away from him?"

By the set of Caleb's chin Libby knew that was exactly what he meant.

Then there was something else Libby knew. She remembered why she liked Caleb. In spite of their disagreement about whether she could go along, they seemed to understand each other. Not since the reporter interviewed him had Libby felt so good just being with Caleb.

Less than an hour later, the *Christina's* whistle blew for Burlington. Near where the gangplank would go down, Libby and Jordan waited.

As the steamboat came about for the landing, Libby glanced down at the river only a foot or so below the edge of the deck. With no railing between her and the water, she was careful to stand back.

From her earliest memory Libby's parents had warned her about the dangers of the narrow strip of water between the boat and shore. More than once she had heard stories about someone who fell in, never to rise again. Though Libby was almost thirteen and tall for her age, the murky depths of the river were well over her head.

Growing more and more impatient, she looked around, searching for Caleb. "Where is he?" she asked Jordan.

But Jordan only shrugged. "We can't look like we is together, you know."

While Libby and Jordan waited, other passengers gathered around. The man closest to the edge of the deck seemed most anxious to leave. Standing with his back to Libby, he wore a hat and long coat in spite of the warmth of the morning. With his highly polished shoes, he looked like a businessman returning home after a trip.

With her deep whistle sounding, the *Christina* drew close to the waterfront. Near Libby, one of the deckhands picked up a landing line. With one end of the rope attached to a cleat on the deck, he wrapped the other end in a coil around his shoulder and elbow.

The moment the gangplank dropped down, the deckhand raced up the plank. In quick, sharp jerks the rope played out behind him.

Again Libby stepped back, but the businessman moved forward. Near the edge of the boat he stood, eagerly looking at the town.

Just then the rope jerked. Snapping tight, it slapped the man across the back of his legs. *Whap!*

Suddenly the man lost his balance. Falling forward, he landed hard, with his stomach hitting the edge of the deck. In the next instant he somersaulted into the dark water between the boat and shore. A moment later he disappeared.

Libby gasped. Had the man's breath been knocked out of him?

Before she could even think what to do, Jordan rushed past her. Kneeling down on the gangplank, he waited.

After what seemed a lifetime, a head rose to the surface—a head with short, closely cut hair. The man's face was turned toward shore.

Jordan called to him, "Here!" Stretching out his hand, Jordan reached across the water.

As though straining toward the sound of Jordan's voice, the man lifted an arm covered with a heavy coat.

His clothes, Libby thought. *His shoes weighing him down. He's got only one chance.*

"Here!" Jordan called again.

As he stretched still farther, Libby gulped. *If he falls in—one slip—*

Quickly Jordan lay down on the gangplank. Again he stretched as far as he could go. This time he grabbed on to the man's hands. With a mighty heave Jordan pulled him up till he lay across the gangplank.

For a moment he clung to the board, trying to catch his breath. Then Jordan stood up and helped the man to his feet. As though unable to stand by himself, the man bent double. Guiding him by the arm, Jordan led him the rest of the way to the *Christina*'s deck.

Even when Jordan let go, the man did not stand up. Still in pain, his shoulders twisted. At last he slowly straightened, facing Jordan.

"It's *you*!" the man exclaimed.

As if he had been burned, the man drew back. Without another word, he stalked off. A moment later he disappeared in the crowd of passengers.

"What an ungrateful person!" Libby exclaimed.

"Maybe," Jordan said calmly.

But Caleb was there now, and Libby told him the whole story. "That man had his breath knocked out. His clothes and shoes weighed him down. He might never have come back up, even a second time."

Listening closely, Caleb agreed with Libby about the man's close call. But Libby was angry now.

"You saved his life, Jordan! And all he said was 'It's *you*!'"

As though it didn't matter, Jordan shrugged aside the whole thing. "Me and Caleb needs to go," he said instead.

Lowering his voice, he spoke to Libby. "We meets you at the farm." Turning, Jordan started down the gangplank.

Then Caleb stood in front of Libby. As she looked into his eyes, Libby knew that moment when she and Caleb seemed to understand each other was gone. Instead, she saw the stiffness that told her Caleb didn't want her along.

When his gaze met hers he said, "Don't take any chances, Libby. We want you back safe."

Then he too was gone.

As Caleb and Jordan started up a Burlington street, Libby watched them go. Each boy carried only a bag on his back. They walked separately, as they usually did when surrounded by people they didn't know. Now and then Caleb turned just slightly, as though keeping an eye on Jordan. Just as often Jordan glanced over toward Caleb.

I hope they're okay, Libby thought. It frightened her just thinking about all the things that could happen to them.

Behind the two boys, other people followed the passengers already on shore. Then roustabouts began unloading freight.

Caleb and Jordan were still in sight when a man hurried past Libby and down the gangplank. The man wore a business suit and hat and seemed familiar. Then, as he reached the first warehouse on the riverfront, he turned just slightly. For the first time Libby saw his face.

The man who fell into the water! The man Jordan rescued!

Libby felt amazed at how fast the man had changed clothes. He was nearly two blocks away when Libby noticed something. *He's not carrying a suitcase or carpetbag. And when he stood near the gangplank he had no baggage.* Yet Libby felt sure the man was leaving the *Christina* for good.

Like a needle poking into her skin, a question jabbed Libby's mind. *Where did he get the dry clothes?*

Her thoughts leaped ahead. *His hair is so short, it would have dried fast.*

Short hair. Hair that has grown. If someone had one side of his head shaved—if it started to grow out, and he cut the other half to match—

The escaped prisoner! The man I saw in Prescott. Sam McGrady!

So! He stole more clothes. Libby wondered which passenger would be angry now. Then she realized something much worse. *If that man is Sam McGrady, he's hurrying up the hill after Caleb and Jordan!*

Without another thought, Libby raced down the gangplank after the boys. By the time she reached the center of town, she was out of breath, and her side ached.

The escaped prisoner was nowhere in sight. Neither were Caleb and Jordan.

Just then Libby heard the *Christina's* final warning bell. She had been so concerned about warning Caleb and Jordan that she hadn't even heard the earlier signals. Now she had no choice but to hurry back to the boat.

"Forty miles to Keokuk," Pa told Libby. "Three and a half hours or so."

Standing on the main deck with people all around them, Pa said no more. But Libby knew what he was talking about.

"If all goes well, you'll meet about the same time," he said quietly.

In the hour before they left the *Christina*, Caleb and Jordan had met in the captain's cabin. Pa had agreed that their plan was a good one—as safe as something like this could be.

Now excitement filled Libby. *I really get to help with Jordan's family!* She still found it hard to believe that she was going along.

Then she looked up at her father. When she saw the love in his eyes, she remembered how Gran felt about Caleb and the Underground Railroad.

"I'll be careful, Pa," Libby promised.

Her father smiled. "Please do. You're the only one I have left."

When a passenger wanted to talk to Pa, Libby searched out Gran in the pastry kitchen. She found Samson there too, sitting on his haunches just outside the door.

"Will you feed him while I'm gone?" Libby asked, and Gran nodded.

Her smile was as warm as her kind blue eyes. "God go with you, Libby."

But when Gran hugged her, Libby knew. Caleb's grandmother already looked forward to that moment when all of them returned.

Standing high on the hurricane deck, Libby looked down over the railing to the river far below. Deep and dark it seemed now, just like the time ahead. Libby wished she could see through to the end—to know that Jordan and his family would reach the *Christina* safely. But the future was filled with dangers Libby could not know. She only knew that she had to listen to Caleb and Jordan and pay attention when Jordan felt uneasy.

More than once since Libby met him, Jordan had felt that uneasiness. Libby knew it was not just a worried feeling, but a lack of God's peace. Both Caleb and Libby had learned to respect the way God gave direction to Jordan.

Libby still felt surprised that Jordan believed God wanted her along. *Why?* she wondered. The day in which Libby thought she could do whatever she set out to do seemed far in the past. Now she had no doubt about all the things she could do wrong.

The whole thing seemed strange to Libby. *Maybe God likes it when people ask for His help.* As she thought about it, she began praying. "Lord, what do you want me to do? Will you show me?"

Then, as if it had happened only a minute before, Libby remembered the day she sat on deck, drawing passengers. When Caleb saw one of her sketches, he said, *"It's good—really good!"*

He had even told Libby, *"Maybe your drawing ability will help us free Jordan's family. I don't know how, but let's think about it."*

Since then, Libby hadn't had much time to think about anything, let alone her drawing. Now she went into her room and took her pencils and drawing paper from her trunk. Then she found a piece of waterproof fabric made of cloth and rubber. Carefully she wrapped it around the paper.

Then Libby put on her jean skirt and her best walking shoes. In a small bag she put the package of paper, her pencils, a warm sweater, and a change of clothes in case she got wet. With that and the food Gran would give her, she was ready for her trip into northeastern Missouri.

When Libby left her room, she climbed the stairs to one of her favorite spots, the pilothouse. Mr. Fletcher, the pilot, stood at one side of the great wheel he used to steer the boat. Because of the wheel's size, it went partway down into the floor.

In front of and above the pilot hung an arrangement of ropes and pulls used to signal the engine far below. Four foot pedals—two whistle and two brake pedals—were in the floor in front of the wheel. At one side, also close to the floor, was a speaking tube.

Sometimes the pilot used bells to signal the engineer. Other times he called down into the tube that was shaped like the end of a trumpet.

Mr. Fletcher turned toward Libby. "Making good time" was all he said before looking back at the river. In the weeks since she had come on board to live with Pa, Fletcher had grown used to her visits.

Libby felt relieved. If anything held them up, their timing would be wrong for meeting Caleb and Jordan at the Missouri farm.

Now Libby gazed down, beyond the bow of the *Christina*. As always, the excitement she felt in the pilothouse flowed into her. With it came her love for the river.

Ahead of them, the waters of the great Mississippi spread wide. Along the shore, the leaves of trees were still bright with the newness of spring.

Before long the channel narrowed. Soon the *Christina* rounded a bend in the river. Not far ahead, directly in her path, lay one of the huge rafts they had seen coming downstream.

When the raft entered a narrow passageway between an island and the riverbank, Libby watched the Red Shirts standing on the two ends of the raft. Each man held one of the long poles used for steering.

Beyond the raft, farther downriver, was a steamboat coming upstream. Suddenly Mr. Fletcher reached out, yanking two bell pulls. Moments later the great paddle wheels reversed, slowing the boat. Fletcher's hands tightened on the wheel.

"That steamboat," he muttered. "The pilot isn't giving the raft enough room."

In the next instant Fletcher leaped onto a brake pedal. With his other foot he slammed down a second pedal. Long and loud the warning whistle shrieked.

"If that steamboat comes too close—" Fletcher's face was grim. Again he sounded a warning. "Suction can pull the raft toward the steamboat. If a chain on the raft breaks—"

Libby didn't have to be told. From what Caleb had said, a chain stretched between each of the logs on the outermost part of the raft. That chain of logs held all the other logs in place.

Again Fletcher yanked the rope signals. Leaning down, he shouted into the speaking tube. "Raft in trouble dead ahead!"

With his foot Fletcher hit the whistle pedal. But the upbound steamboat paid no attention. Closer and closer it came. As though determined to have his way, the pilot held his course.

Suddenly the raft pulled to the left. Fletcher gritted his teeth. "The suction got 'em!"

10

Peddler Paul

As if the suction was growing stronger, the raft moved faster and faster. Working frantically, the Red Shirts swept the oars. But the long poles did little good.

Suddenly an outside log on the raft broke loose. As the chain of logs broke apart, more logs spun off. One after another they shot out in all directions.

Then an entire section of the raft split away. The man who stood on it jumped across the widening stretch of water to a larger piece of raft. With the Red Shirts no longer able to steer, the raft slipped directly into the path of the upcoming boat.

On the *Christina* warning bells clanged. More and more logs broke loose. Again Fletcher blew the whistle.

Our hull! Libby thought in panic. In spite of Fletcher's efforts, the *Christina* was coming up on a piece of raft. Even one of the huge logs could break a hole in the wooden hull. In a matter of minutes, the *Christina* would fill with water and go down.

In the next instant Fletcher spun the wheel hard to the right. Trying to find a way around the logs, he sought open water between them and the nearby shore.

Just then the upcoming boat poured on steam. Swinging out

around the logs spreading in all directions, the boat managed to slip past them.

"That steamboat is leaving!" Libby cried out. "The pilot caused the accident, and he's leaving!"

Fletcher was so busy avoiding logs that he paid no attention. Beads of perspiration broke out on his lips as he steered so close to the shore that Libby feared they would run aground.

As the first log bumped against the hull, Libby's stomach tightened. From where she stood, Libby heard only a soft thud, but she knew the impact could be much worse than it sounded.

Then came another thud and another. Desperately Fletcher worked to keep from bearing down on the remaining sections of the raft. Desperately he worked to keep from striking the men trying to steer the broken segments toward shore.

When at last Libby felt the difference in thuds, she breathed deeply. Now she could see what was happening. The *Christina* had slowed enough so the logs began drifting downstream, away from them.

On the wheel Fletcher flexed the fingers of his hands, then tightened them again. As the *Christina* drew close to one of the larger segments, he leaned out the window to listen.

Far below Captain Norstad stood on the forward deck. He called to one of the men. "Want some help?"

Instantly the anger in the man's face disappeared. Libby knew the anger was for the other steamboat, and she felt the same way. Yet she couldn't help but wonder if she would be too late for the peddler in Keokuk.

"Thank you, sir!" the Red Shirt called back. "Any help you'd like to give."

"Let's round up the big sections first," Captain Norstad called. "At least you'll save some of the logs."

Starting with the large broken segment closest to them, Fletcher steered the *Christina*, gently nudging the edge of the raft with the bow. As that part of the raft rode the water toward another segment of logs, men reached out, grabbing hold. Working quickly, they bound the two segments together.

Careful to not come too close, Fletcher guided the *Christina* slowly ahead. Wherever the pilot could reach a section of logs with the bow, he did. When the largest sections were rounded up, the Red Shirts made them fast along the shore.

Some of the individual logs had drifted against the riverbank, catching on trees. Other logs had escaped downstream. Libby had no doubt that without the *Christina*'s help the man responsible for the raft would have lost thousands of dollars. Even so, his loss would be great.

When at last the *Christina* had done all she could, Fletcher waved to the men.

"A million thank-yous!" a Red Shirt called out. A cheer went up from the rest of them.

Before long Captain Norstad entered the *Christina*'s pilothouse. "Good work!" he said, clapping Fletcher on the shoulder.

Libby felt proud of both Fletcher and Pa. They had done the best they could in a bad situation. But on her way down the stairs, Libby thought about Caleb and Jordan again. Jordan's plan would fall apart if their timing wasn't right.

When she reached the large main cabin Libby stared at the clock. It was even worse than she feared. *What if the peddler doesn't wait? What if he thinks no one is coming?*

Carrying only a small bag on her back, Libby left the *Christina* at Keokuk, Iowa. Pa walked beside her up the steep hill to the marketplace. There, in the center of town, Pa tipped his head toward a peddler's wagon.

The wagon was eight or ten feet long. The high black sides and covered top were large enough to protect the great number of boxes, drawers, and shelves that held whatever the peddler wanted to sell. On the almost flat top were more wooden boxes. Buckets, brooms, and all kinds of farming tools hung wherever possible.

The peddler stood next to his wagon, talking with whoever came by. But he gave no sign that he had seen Libby or her father.

Captain Norstad kept walking, passing by on the other side of the street as if the wagon was of no interest to him. Half a block farther on, Pa said, "The peddler is well known in this area. People like him. Most of them don't know he also works for the Underground Railroad."

When Libby glanced back she saw the peddler putting away his wares. She and Pa were at least a block away when the peddler climbed up to the seat at the front of the wagon.

At the next corner Captain Norstad turned. Two blocks beyond that, on a quiet, tree-lined street, Libby was surprised to see the peddler's wagon had gone around them on another street, then stopped. "God go with you, Libby," Pa said softly as they drew near to the wagon. "Be careful, won't you?"

Half scared and half excited, Libby nodded. After talking with Gran, it wasn't hard for her to guess how hard this must be for Pa.

"I'll be very careful," she said. "We'll do our best to meet you in Burlington four days from now."

The man waiting on the high wooden seat had a long gray beard and gray hair that hung down over the collar of his coat. Reins in hand, he seemed ready to leave on a moment's notice.

"Paul, this is my daughter," Pa said softly.

"I'll take good care of her, Captain," the man promised.

As Libby climbed up to the high seat, the man lifted his hat to-ward Pa. Beneath bushy eyebrows, his eyes were sharp and alert. "The Lord bless and keep you, Captain."

When Paul called "Giddyup!" to the horses, Libby twisted around to look back. The place where she sat was under an over-hang to protect the driver in all kinds of weather. Through a small square opening in the end of the wagon, she watched Pa disappear in the distance. Until then Libby hadn't realized how hard it would be to leave him. But she had the feeling that Pa and the peddler had been friends for a long time.

"Did you have trouble?" Paul asked as he and Libby passed out of town.

"A raft broke loose. Logs scattered all over the river. Pa needed to stop and help."

"Did the logs hurt the *Christina*?"

Libby shook her head. "But it could have been really bad."

"I was told to look for Caleb and a fugitive," Paul said. "I wasn't expecting you."

Libby grinned. "I wasn't expecting me either."

She explained about the escaped prisoner and the need for a change in plans. When she told Paul about Jordan's plan for a midnight rescue, Paul said, "I've been to the Weaver farm often."

After a time Paul asked about Caleb. "Is he all right?"

"As far as I know, Caleb is safe." In spite of their differences, Libby liked and admired him. Her voice grew soft with even the mention of his name.

As though sensing the change in Libby's voice, Paul glanced her way. "We've made lots of trips together, Caleb and I."

"Do you know him well?" Libby asked. She wanted to learn everything she could about Caleb.

Paul smiled. "I know him the way a man knows a man, instead of the way a man knows a boy. Caleb grew up too fast. But he's earned the respect of everyone who knows him."

Strange, Libby thought. She had always felt that Caleb seemed older than his age. But every now and then something else broke through—the thirteen-year-old boy that was there, after all. The boy who teased her and knew how to have a good time.

Then a tight knot formed around Libby's heart. Once she had felt sure that Caleb liked her. Now she didn't feel sure about anything. *Caleb knows how I failed. He didn't want me along.*

When Libby described the place where Caleb wanted to meet, Paul said, "I know exactly where he means. If all goes well, we can still be there by one o'clock or so."

For a while Paul followed the red arrows painted on trees to mark the way. When the road led them close to a good-sized river, Libby learned it was the Des Moines. The wide stream flowed at a southeast angle to join the Mississippi River below Keokuk. Libby knew that every creek and river they needed to cross would be a barrier on their way back from northeastern Missouri.

Soon Paul began telling Libby about his life as a peddler—how he wandered up and down the often muddy roads in all kinds of weather. All through the spring, summer, and autumn he sought out people who needed what he wanted to sell. Only in winter did he stay home to protect his horses from trying to get through deep snow.

During the day Paul stopped at every farmhouse he passed. At night he wrapped his blanket around him and slept under the wagon.

"And you, Libby?" Paul's long gray beard rose and fell in the breeze. He wanted to hear about her life on the *Christina*.

To her own surprise Libby soon felt comfortable with Paul. After the dangerous things that had happened on the boat, she welcomed this peaceful time. Whenever Libby tried to think ahead, her stomach knotted with nervousness.

At St. Francisville Paul got down and led the horses onto a ferry. When the wagon rolled off the ferry on the other side of the Des Moines River, he said, "We're in Missouri now."

In the flat bottomland next to the river, the soil looked black and good. As the land became more hilly, Libby and Paul rode past great stretches of timber.

"It's hard work," Paul said, and Libby wondered what he meant. He stretched out his hand to the woods.

"Oak, maple, and walnut trees. Cottonwood and birch along the streams. It's God's country, but hard work to clear. Lots of southern people settled here—owners bringing their slaves along. Down south slaves were used to gentler ways—picking cotton instead of clearing land. It gives them an extra reason for running."

Gentler ways. Libby thought about Paul's words. To her the land was beautiful. She liked the tall trees, the road leading up a hill, then sharply down. She liked the valleys, the deep ravines, the yellow buttercups along the creeks. But she didn't have to cut down the trees, clear out the stumps, and plant a crop.

Now Libby could barely see enough. Wherever she looked, there were wild flowers under the trees. Paul told her their names— violets and sweet William, boy britches and May apples.

Like the budding out of flowers after a long winter, hope stirred within Libby. Would this be springtime for Jordan's family? *Maybe—just maybe, I can do something to help them after all.*

But then Paul stopped the horses in front of a large poster nailed to a tree. The top line of letters was large enough for people to read as they passed by.

Negroes for Sale

When Paul climbed down from the wagon, Libby followed him. In smaller letters, she read the rest of the notice:

A WOMAN,

who is a fine cook,

washer and ironer,

having been raised to that business.

Also, one boy, eight years old,

an eleven-year-old girl, trained for housework,

and a young child, sound and healthy.

As though she could not believe what she read, Libby felt sick inside. "The description fits them perfectly. That's Jordan's mother and Serena and Zack and little Rose!"

Libby stared at the owner's name on the bottom of the poster. "Jordan knew something was wrong. Something worse than usual, I mean."

Tears rose in Libby's throat. Unable to face the poster, she turned away. When she climbed back into the wagon, her tears spilled over and ran down her cheeks.

"What if Jordan's family is sold before he gets there?" Libby asked as Paul drove on. "Jordan will never find them again!"

"Would they go with us if we get there in time?"

"I doubt it," Libby answered. "Jordan said his mother won't trust just anyone. She's heard too many stories about runaway slaves who get caught. She and Jordan have an agreement between them that he'll come back to help her."

"Maybe Jordan and Caleb are ahead of us now." Paul clucked to the horses and slapped the reins across their backs.

After a time Paul slowed the horses. "We're almost there," he said.

Looking ahead, Libby saw a creek. Before reaching it, Paul turned the horses off the road. In a wide space between trees, he drove into the woods. When he stopped, Libby could still see the road, but they were somewhat hidden from whoever might drive by.

Unhitching the horses, Paul led them down to water. As they drank, he took out a pocket watch. "We're right on time, and this is where we're supposed to meet."

When the horses finished drinking, he led them to a place where they could graze.

Libby climbed down from the wagon and sat with her back against the trunk of a tree. As an hour slipped away, Libby grew more and more anxious. *Where are you, Caleb?* she wanted to cry out. *Has something happened to you and Jordan?*

The questions kept going around and around in her mind. In her mind's eye she could still see the man Jordan rescued from the water. The man Libby believed to be the Stillwater prisoner. With each passing minute she felt more upset. *It's my fault. I should have found Caleb and Jordan. I should have warned them.* It did little good to tell herself that she had done her best.

Then Libby realized what she was doing—slipping into her old way of thinking. She remembered Gran's words. *"Being a Christian doesn't mean that all your problems are gone. It means that you have Jesus to help you in everything you face."*

Opening the bag she carried on her back, Libby took out her drawing paper and pencils. Under the trees were the waxy white flowers Paul called May apples, and Libby sketched them quickly.

A short distance away, where the sun shone between the trees, Libby found violets.

"Don't go too far," Paul called to her. "The Fox River outlaws hide out around here."

"The Fox River *outlaws*?"

"Bands of thieves. They've got a lot of good hiding places in these woods. That's why I keep a close watch on the horses. There have been so many horses stolen in this area that a man by the name of David McKee finally said 'Enough is enough!' He formed the Anti-Horse Thief Association."

"So now, in the midst of an impossible rescue, we have to watch out for horse thieves?"

Paul grinned. "Don't you worry. We'll make it through."

By the time Libby finished drawing the violets, she found that even Paul had grown restless. "Caleb and Jordan are over two hours late," he said.

By now it was almost three o'clock. When Paul took food from the wagon, Libby unwrapped one of the sandwiches Gran had given her. Libby felt sure the bread and cheese were as good as usual. But Libby's scared feelings turned the sandwich into something dry and tasteless.

As they finished eating, she heard a splashing sound from the creek. Moments later a boy of about eight appeared. Over his shoulder he carried a fishing pole with one small fish on the line.

"Jonathan!" Paul exclaimed. "How are you doing?"

The boy grinned at him. "So you're back. I thought it was time. My ma and sis will be right glad to see you. All winter long they've been making lists of what to buy."

"I expect so," Paul said. But he did not move from the stump where he sat.

"What are you waiting for?" Jonathan asked. Walking around the wagon, he peered at every side, though Paul had opened only one of the doors.

"I wish Zack was here to see you," Jonathan said as he finished his inspection of the wagon.

"Zack?" Paul asked. According to Jordan, Zack was about eight years old.

"Me and Zack have a secret meeting place," Jonathan answered. "He's an honorary member of my club—the only boy I know who doesn't tell me I'm fat."

When Paul's gaze met Libby's, she guessed what he was thinking. *Zack isn't sold yet.*

A shadow passed over Jonathan's face. "Pa says Zack is old enough to work in the fields now. All day long he's hoeing corn and carrying water. It ain't any fun when he's not here."

Jonathan leaned his pole against a tree and sat down. "No more fishing for Zack, except on Sundays. Ma says Sundays is meant for boys to sit quiet and still. But Zack's ma lets him fish as soon as he comes from church. She says it's the only day of the week Zack can fish, and the good Lord made fishing for boys."

Soon Jonathan looked restless again. "Yesterday Pa said he needs to see you, Mr. Martin. Needs some new tools, I guess. I'll run tell him you're here." Standing up, Jonathan grabbed his pole and was off.

"No, wait," Paul called after him. "We'll rest a bit more and come later."

But Jonathan was already headed for the road and the bridge

across the creek. Before he slipped out of sight, he called to them. "I'm the fastest runner there is!"

"What do we do now?" Libby asked, the dread within her growing.

"We'll water our horses as long as we possibly can," Paul said. "But I wish Caleb would come. There are a lot of slave catchers who know what he's up to."

"Along the Iowa border?" Libby asked.

"In that whole area he has to cross," Paul told her. "Caleb is one of our best conductors. He's had to take a lot of risks and hasn't lost a passenger yet. But today I keep thinking about his grandmother."

Gran. She too knew the risks for Caleb. What would happen to Caleb if he was caught? But for Jordan it would be even worse. *If he's sent back to that cruel slave trader who owns him, Jordan will lose more than his freedom. Riggs might even beat him to death.*

And Jordan's family. What would happen to them?

Much sooner than Paul and Libby wanted, Jonathan was back, shouting at them from across the creek.

"Pa says to come right away. He needs to see you now. Says he has to talk with a big important man tomorrow."

11

Family Spy

*T*urning, Jonathan headed back into the trees. His legs flew, as though he wanted to see the excitement when Paul arrived. But the peddler took his time about hitching up his horses.

Soon after Libby and Paul returned to the road, the horses brought them to a bridge made from heavy logs thrown down across the creek. As they passed beyond the wooded area, Libby looked across an open field. A tall, stately home stood on a rise.

"What a beautiful house!" Libby exclaimed.

The main part of the house was built of red brick. The front porch had tall white pillars that extended upward to another porch on the second floor. On this side of the house and toward the back were two more even larger upper and lower porches. An open stairway led between them.

"Better put on your thinking cap," Paul told Libby as they continued toward the driveway. "If Caleb and Jordan don't get here soon, we need lots of reasons for staying around."

But Libby was still studying the lay of the land. On the south side of the long driveway was a tin-roofed barn and smaller outbuildings. Between those buildings and the field behind the house were what Paul said were slave cabins. Built of logs, they looked as though they had one tiny room. Seeing the cabins, Libby started to wonder about the dogs owned by the Weaver family.

It didn't take long to find them. The moment Paul turned into the driveway, the dogs began barking. Yipping and jumping up, they raced out to meet the peddler's wagon. With their long droopy ears and wrinkled faces, they reminded Libby of worried old men.

Then she remembered. *They're not like Samson. They're not just family pets. Those dogs are bloodhounds trained to track down runaway slaves.*

Paying no attention to the dogs, Paul wrapped the reins around a post on the wagon. Taking out a flute, he played a cheerful song meant to draw everyone who heard.

In the field behind the house, two black men lifted their heads. Resting their hands on their hoes, they listened. On the shaded front porch, a blond girl about Libby's age jumped up.

Paul called to her. "Tell your mother!"

At the side door of the house, Jonathan stood waiting. To Libby's surprise one of the bloodhounds ran up to him. When Jonathan reached down to pet him, the dog waited for a scratch behind his ears.

The minute Jonathan saw Libby, he waved as if the two were old friends. But Jordan's brother, Zack, was not with him.

Where is he? Libby wondered, wanting to make sure Zack truly was still around. She saw no one who looked like an eight-year-old Jordan. Then Libby remembered. Zack would be working in the fields all day.

Outside the white picket fence that surrounded the house, Paul called, "Whoa!" From every direction people gathered around. Young and old, black and white, they all seemed curious about the peddler's wagon.

Soon a black woman came through the opening in the picket fence. Tall and slender, she wore a white apron as if she worked in the house. *Could that be Jordan's mother, Hattie?* Close behind was a girl who looked just a bit younger than Libby. *Eleven-year-old Serena,* Libby decided.

From the direction of the slave cabins ran a string of children, followed by the old woman who cared for them. Serena stopped and waited, then picked up one of the children. The little girl had pigtails sticking out all over her head and seemed about fifteen months old. Libby felt sure she was Jordan's youngest sister, Rose.

As Libby watched, Rose threw her arms around Serena's neck. Serena hugged the little girl to herself. More than once Serena whispered something in her ear. When Rose giggled, Serena giggled too.

Is that what it means to have a sister? Libby wondered. *No wonder Jordan wants to rescue his family!*

To Libby's surprise Paul climbed down from the wagon slowly, as if his aging bones hurt. Even in the way Paul opened his wagon he took his time.

Then Libby remembered. *He's giving Caleb and Jordan every minute he can.* In her thoughts she wished she could hurry them on. *Where are you?* she wanted to cry out.

On one side of the wagon, Paul folded down a shelf. On that he put his most valuable items—glassware, china dishes, and patent medicines in their thick glass bottles. Next to that he set a jar of hard candy.

From the back of the wagon, he took out long pieces of cloth, pots and pans, and all that would appeal to a woman. When he set those on another shelf where they could be easily viewed, the eager children and grown-ups gathered close.

Soon a woman who appeared to be Jonathan's mother came through the opening in the picket fence. A boy about two years old was with her, along with a blond girl who seemed to be Jonathan's sister.

"Hello, Mrs. Weaver," Paul said warmly. "And how may I help you today?"

A smile lit her face. "I know it's spring when you come back to us again," she said. "I need cloth, as usual, for the dresses we need to sew. Thread and buttons. And if you'll sharpen my scissors and knives—"

Paul nodded. "And what about some china?" He pointed to the dishes on the shelf he had opened. "Bone china of the best quality. Imported all the way from England. Sure to please your most particular guests."

Drawing close to the wagon, Mrs. Weaver picked up a cup and read the name on the bottom. As she held the cup to the light, Libby remembered that Paul wanted excuses for them to stay longer. While Paul and Mrs. Weaver bargained about the price of the china,

Libby took out her drawings of wild flowers and set them on the seat. Then she began sketching the young boy who clung to Mrs. Weaver's skirt.

As Libby drew the boy's round cheek, she watched the others gathered around. The girl Libby thought to be Serena stood near the back. Her curly black hair tucked under a scarf, she wore a white apron as though she too worked in the house.

I wish I could talk to her, Libby thought. *I wish I could ask her name.* Instead she kept drawing the young boy. By the time Paul and Mrs. Weaver agreed on the price of the china, Libby had finished sketching the boy's eyes and nose.

Mrs. Weaver turned. "Serena!" Instantly the girl with the white apron put down the younger child.

She is *Jordan's sister!* Libby thought.

As Serena walked forward her bare feet picked up the dust. Coming to stand next to Mrs. Weaver, she waited with her gaze on the ground.

When Mrs. Weaver asked Serena to carry the china to the house, she and the tall black woman made several trips. After Mrs. Weaver purchased a great amount of cloth, the girl Libby had seen on the porch stepped forward.

"Melanie would like some necklaces," Mrs. Weaver said.

Her daughter's long hair was gathered back and held up with a ribbon, much the way Libby's was. But Melanie's eyes looked unhappy, as if she were bored with life. Instead of choosing between necklaces, she wanted nearly all of them.

As the waiting children grew restless, Paul spoke to them. "When we're all done, I'll have a piece of candy for each of you."

When the younger children drew closer, Serena held back, as if not sure she was included. But Paul saw her.

"I have enough for all of you," he said.

When at last Melanie made up her mind, she turned. "Serena!"

Her gaze still on the ground, Serena stepped forward. When she held out both hands, Melanie hung the necklaces over Serena's wrists. Keeping her arms out, away from her apron, Serena held the long chains carefully.

"Take the necklaces to my room," Melanie said.

For one instant Serena's glance flicked toward Paul, as though thinking about his promise of candy. Then she started away.

"Serena, is it?" Paul called after her. "I'll still be here when you come back."

With careful steps Serena started toward the house. *I wonder what would happen if she dropped one of the necklaces*, Libby thought.

Afraid that she would show her feelings to Melanie and Mrs. Weaver, Libby looked down. Her sketch was coming nicely now, and Libby filled in the boy's eyelashes. Glancing back and forth between him and the paper, Libby drew his lips.

Just then Mrs. Weaver noticed Libby's wild-flower sketches. "These are *good*!" she exclaimed. "May apples and violets. Just the way they look in our spring woods!"

"Thank you," Libby said quietly. Always she had felt grateful for the art lessons she'd had. But she also felt surprised whenever someone liked her drawings.

"Are these for sale?" Mrs. Weaver asked.

Startled, Libby glanced toward Paul.

"Indeed they are," he said quickly. "It's a talented artist I have with me, don't you think?"

Not sure whether Paul was teasing or not, Libby looked down. Her drawing of the boy was nearly finished.

"Ohhh!" Mrs. Weaver's exclamation broke into Libby's thoughts. "My son, Randolph! You did this just now?"

When Libby nodded, Mrs. Weaver turned to Paul. "Let's decide on a price for the wild-flower sketches."

As soon as they settled on an amount, Mrs. Weaver turned back to Libby. "I used to do quite a bit of oil painting. Will you do two more sketches—one of Jonathan and one of Melanie?"

By now Melanie had left, but Libby smiled at the boy she had already met. Jonathan would be fun to draw, but Melanie? Libby dreaded it. More than once she had been too honest about the way someone looked.

I'll have to change the unhappiness in Melanie's eyes, Libby decided.

"When you finish your sketch of Jonathan, will you bring it to the house?" Mrs. Weaver asked. "I'll talk to my husband about having you draw all of us—the entire family together."

Inwardly Libby gulped. *I can't do that*, she thought. But when she looked toward Paul, he blinked his eyes as though saying yes.

"Now I must go," Mrs. Weaver said. "When you're finished with the drawings, I'll pay you for your work. My husband likes to have his dinner on time."

As Mrs. Weaver started toward the house, Libby saw a man at the side door. With his hair combed back and every strand in place, he wore a three-piece suit. When he lifted his hand toward Paul, the peddler nodded. Then Mr. Weaver disappeared into the house.

Paul waited until Serena returned before offering the rest of the children their candy. When Serena again held back, he said, "Come, come. Enough for all of you."

Taking the jar from where the children had watched it all this time, Paul lifted the cover. As each child held up a hand, Paul put one piece of candy in an open palm.

Serena was the last to come forward. When Paul tipped the jar, his hand moved quickly, closing around two pieces of candy. When Serena stretched out her hands, he dropped both pieces into her open palms. Instantly Serena's fist closed around them.

No one else saw, Libby thought.

For a moment Serena's eyes flicked upward. "Thank you, Mr. Martin," she said softly. Not even her eyes gave away the knowledge that she had been given two pieces of candy instead of one. Then Serena turned toward the house.

Later when Paul was sharpening knives, Serena slipped back to the wagon. Quietly she stood watching his nimble fingers and the sparks flying off the grindstone. With no one else around, she waited for Paul's wheel to slow down enough for her to speak softly.

"What's you want me to know, Mr. Martin?" she asked.

Instantly alert, Libby listened. Had the two pieces of candy been some kind of code between them? Pa had said that Paul worked with the Underground Railroad.

When he spoke Paul did not look toward Serena. With his gaze still on the knife he was sharpening, he said, "Tell your momma to listen for a signal."

As if the morning sun had risen within her, a glow spread across

Serena's face. Then, just as quickly as it came, the glow disappeared. Serena's face went blank.

Turning, she raced through the gate and up the path to the house.

The minute the evening meal was over, Jonathan came back to the wagon. Eager to have his picture drawn, he sat down on the stool Libby gave him.

From one direction, then another, Libby studied him. Finally, after moving him around a bit, she started drawing. She had only a few lines on paper when Mr. Weaver came out to the wagon.

Paul greeted the man politely, but Libby heard the stiffness in the peddler's voice. When Mr. Weaver started haggling about the price of farm tools, Libby again sensed the difference in the way Paul felt.

Finally Mr. Weaver went back to the house, and Libby continued sketching. Soon she realized there was something wrong with the drawing. Jonathan did not look the way he should. At last Libby had to give up.

"What's wrong?" the boy asked when Libby tore up the paper.

"You just don't look right," Libby said.

Jonathan giggled. "There's lots of people who say that."

"That's not what I mean." A flush of embarrassment warmed Libby's cheeks. "You look right. I just can't make you look the way you do."

Again Jonathan thought she was being funny. When he laughed Libby decided what was wrong. She wanted to show the happy way he looked at the creek. "Jonathan, can you get your fishing pole and hold it over your shoulder?" she asked.

"Well, I don't know. I don't think Pa will like that picture," he said.

"Let's try it anyway," Libby said.

When Jonathan returned, he carried the pole over his shoulder with the dead fish still hanging from its line. Libby wondered how soon the fish would start to smell.

This time the drawing went well. Partway through, Libby began asking questions.

"Jonathan, you know that boy who's an honorary member of your club? I don't think I've seen him. Where is he?"

"Working." Jonathan's expression told Libby what he thought of that. "Working till the sun goes down."

"In the field?" Libby asked. The field in front of the house had no workers. Would Zack be in the field on the back side?

Jonathan pointed that way.

"And that's where your secret meeting place is too?" Libby asked.

"Shucks, no. Me and Zack hides under the bridge." Jonathan glanced toward the creek and the road leading to the place where Paul and Libby stopped. "There's a wide spot under the bridge—a dirt bank where we sit without getting wet. Zack tells me stories there."

By the time Jonathan started getting wiggly, Libby was far enough to let him go. When at last she finished the drawing, she felt pleased with it. Jonathan looked like he was ready for fun.

When Libby started toward the big house, she wasn't sure whether to go to the side, back, or front door. Stopping, she felt afraid to go on. Then she thought about it. *If I were a professional artist, I wouldn't sneak around feeling scared. I would march right up to the front door.*

As Libby reached the porch with tall pillars, Melanie came out the door. Her eyes still looked unhappy, even resentful.

"Go on in," she said when Libby asked for Melanie's parents. "They're in the living room."

Inside the front door Libby found a hallway with stairs leading upward. Straight ahead, another door led to the back porch. On Libby's left she saw the living room through a partly opened door.

On the far wall was a fireplace with a fire crackling against the dampness of the evening. Beyond that a tall window stretched from a few feet above the floor to the twelve-foot ceiling. Long drapes hung on either side of the window and nearby was a door. In front of the fire, Mr. and Mrs. Weaver sat with their backs toward Libby.

She was about to knock on the doorpost when Mr. Weaver spoke. "I have a buyer for Zack," he said.

Instead of knocking, Libby lowered her hand and listened.

"You're selling *Zack*?" Mrs. Weaver sounded upset. "You didn't tell me about that."

"I'm telling you now."

"But Hattie's husband and one son have already been sold away from her."

So, Libby thought, remembering the poster nailed to the tree. *Mr. Weaver hasn't told his wife that he plans to sell* all *of Jordan's family. He must still be looking for buyers for Hattie and the girls.*

Across the room, a mirror hung at just the right angle for Libby to see the pain in Mrs. Weaver's face. "You'll break Hattie's heart if you tear another son from her arms," she said. "You can't do that to her."

"I didn't sell her husband." Mr. Weaver sounded resentful. "I didn't sell her older boy."

"Of course you didn't. But someone did."

"We've never had a slave who cared so much about our children," Mrs. Weaver went on. "When I was sick she took care of little Randolph day and night. He would have died if she hadn't watched and fed him."

But Mr. Weaver shook his head. "It's no use, Dorothy. I bought more land. I have to pay for it."

Tears stood in Mrs. Weaver's eyes. "You used to love our people. What has happened to change you so?"

Mr. Weaver sighed. "I never seem to be able to give you enough."

"Enough of what?"

"Money. Fine things."

Mrs. Weaver's eyes looked startled. "But you never asked me. Is that what you think I want? Did I tell you that's what I wanted?"

Then a pinched look came into her face. "I did, didn't I? The day before Melanie was born, I compared our home with what my father had after thirty years of hard work. But when I changed I never told you."

Before Libby's eyes, Mrs. Weaver's face seemed to grow old. "I'm as guilty as you," she told her husband. "And now, all I really want is you and our children. I want a home and the food and clothes they need. But all this—"

Mrs. Weaver stretched out her hand, taking in the furniture and paintings. "We could sell this instead of Zack. We don't need it."

Mr. Weaver looked around the living room. "You would sell something you painted yourself? And the furniture you brought from the South? Who would pay us what they're really worth? The man coming tomorrow wants Zack as a companion for his son."

With angry eyes Mrs. Weaver stared at her husband. "Zack is best friends with *our* son."

Mr. Weaver's voice was hard. "The boy has to go," he said.

As if she couldn't bear to look at her husband, Mrs. Weaver bowed her head and covered her eyes. When the sound of weeping filled the room, Libby inched forward. Again she noticed the long full drapes at the far window. In that moment one of the drapes moved.

12

Nighttime Visit

*W*hen Mrs. Weaver continued crying, Mr. Weaver leaned toward his wife. "There, there, Dorothy," he muttered as if embarrassed by her tears.

For the first time Libby saw the man's face in the mirror. Cold and angry he seemed, in spite of his words.

When Mrs. Weaver looked up, her eyes were red from crying. "We've taken so many wrong turns. To rob Hattie of her son would be the greatest wrong of all."

"We don't have any choice, Dorothy. The land I bought has to be paid for, or we'll lose what we already have."

"There's nothing I can say to change your mind?"

"Nothing, Dorothy. Absolutely nothing. The boy goes in the morning."

As the sound of weeping once more filled the room, Libby started to edge backward. She needed to get away before someone discovered her. But just then the long drape moved again. As Libby watched, a boy's hand pushed aside the cloth. Then a face appeared. *Jonathan!*

For a moment he waited, as though making sure that his parents looked the other way. Then he slipped out the nearby door.

Again Libby edged back. As she crept toward the front door, her feelings tumbled every which way. Without making a sound, she opened the door and stepped outside.

By the time Libby reached Paul, she was shaking with anger one minute and trembling with fear the next. Stumbling over her words, she struggled to make sense of what she was trying to say. "Jonathan knows what is going to happen to his best friend."

In the silence that followed, Paul offered Libby a bench. As though needing time to think, he lit a lantern and set it down on another bench.

"What should we do?" Libby asked finally.

"You need to go back," he said. "See if they want you to draw a family picture in the morning."

"I'm supposed to draw another picture at a time like this?"

"Maybe you will. Maybe you won't," Paul answered. "Just show them your sketch of Jonathan and see what Mr. Weaver says."

"But, Paul—" Libby couldn't get the terrible scene in the living room out of her mind. "I can't go back to that room."

"If Jordan asked you to walk into that room, would you do it?"

Libby stared at Paul. "I guess I would," she said slowly.

"Why?"

Libby thought about it. "Because it's Jordan's family that's being torn apart. But it's more. Jordan has always known he would lead his people to freedom. From the time he was a little boy, his momma told him so. And God told Jordan too."

"Then let's try to get more time for Jordan," Paul said. "We don't know why he's not here. Whatever is wrong, it has to be a good reason."

"But what about Jordan's mother?" Libby said. "She needs to get Zack and run away tonight. We could take her."

"Maybe," Paul said. "But for now go and talk to the Weavers before they go to bed. Maybe Jordan will come while you're gone."

Libby was still filled with dread. There was something she needed to know. "When Jordan prayed with Caleb and me, he asked God for favor. What does that mean?"

"A couple of things," Paul answered. "If you do something well, someone might like what you did. That's human favor."

"The way Mrs. Weaver liked my drawings."

Paul nodded. "But when God gives favor, it's much more than that. He blesses you, not because you earn or deserve it, but because of the way He is. God just likes to bless people. He wants to help us."

Reaching down, Paul picked up the lantern. "Whether this flame is lit depends on something you do. You light it or don't light it. If you do something people like, they might choose to give you favor. But God's favor is like the sun. God does not turn off the sun. Sometimes clouds block our view of it, but the sun is still there."

"Then we better pray for favor," Libby said. "Both kinds of favor."

Once more she picked up her sketch of Jonathan. In the light of the lantern, the dead fish almost looked alive. Seeing it, Libby felt better. Then she noticed the twinkle in Paul's eyes.

"Remember, Libby. You're a professional artist now. You've already sold two drawings of wild flowers and one of Randolph."

As Libby walked toward the house, she made all the noise she could. When she reached the front door, she did not go in. Instead she knocked loudly. When Serena answered she led Libby into the living room.

Mr. and Mrs. Weaver still sat in front of a fire that had now burned low. The redness in Mrs. Weaver's eyes had not gone away. Yet, if Libby had not heard them talking, she might not have sensed their disagreement.

"I finished the drawing of Jonathan," Libby said, hoping she could soon be out of there.

When Mrs. Weaver took it, she held it out at arm's length. Without speaking, she studied the sketch.

"What is it?" her husband asked.

Mrs. Weaver looked up to meet Libby's gaze. "It's our son Jonathan at his best—when he is happy."

Standing up, Mr. Weaver looked over his wife's shoulder. "At his best with a fish over his shoulder?"

"Yes." Mrs. Weaver's smile was soft, as if knowing that Libby understood. "You have given us more than you know," Mrs. Weaver told her. "We want to buy this drawing from you."

Then, as if remembering the conversation Libby had heard, Mrs. Weaver paused. "But I want to give you something better than money—something my father gave me long ago on the day I sold my first painting."

Carefully Mrs. Weaver unclasped a bracelet from around her wrist. She handed it to Libby.

"But you can't—" her husband began.

"Yes, I can. It is mine. Now it is Libby's. She has reminded me of something important."

Mrs. Weaver glanced at her husband. "We haven't talked about it yet," she told Libby. "But in the morning, right after breakfast, we want you to make a drawing of our entire family. We will sit for you in front of our house. You may arrange us as you like."

As Libby left the room, she did not dare to look at Mr. Weaver.

When Libby reached Paul again, she found that he had moved as many boxes as possible so that Libby could make a bed inside the wagon. His bedroll lay on the ground a short distance away.

When Libby showed him the bracelet, Paul looked surprised. "It's very valuable. Take good care of it. Mrs. Weaver comes from a wealthy Southern family."

Much as Mrs. Weaver's kindness meant to her, Libby was more concerned about Caleb and Jordan. "Did they come while I was gone?"

Paul shook his head. "I don't want to worry, but I feel concerned."

"Paul—" Libby had already thought through her plan. "I think I know where Jordan's mother sleeps. When I waited in the front hall, I looked through a door into the porch off the kitchen. I saw slaves going up a stairway there. The women looked like they work in the house."

"It would make sense," Paul said. "Slaves who work in the house usually do live there. But their part of the house would be separate from where the family lives."

"And Serena and Rose?"

"Probably with Hattie. But Zack would be in a cabin out back."

"You think I should talk to Jordan's mother?"

"If you do, there are probably two rooms for slaves. You can't make a mistake about which one she's in."

Suddenly the whole prospect of what lay ahead frightened Libby. When she crept into her bed in the wagon, she wanted to do nothing. If she waited long enough, maybe Jordan and Caleb would come.

One by one the lamps in the big house went out. Through an opening between boards in the wagon, Libby watched the house grow dark.

With it came the growing sense that she had no choice but to do something. She remembered Jordan's words. *"If Caleb and I can't get there, Momma will have another chance to escape."* It would be the worst unkindness of all to not tell Hattie what was happening.

Finally Libby could lie still no longer. Leaving her shoes in the wagon, she climbed down. "I'm going," she told Paul. "If the dogs start barking—"

"They're in the barn," Paul said. "All except one. I've come so often that he knows me. He's Jonathan's pet."

Staying within the shadows, Libby crept around the back side of the house. There she waited until her eyes grew used to the darkness. Then, rounding the corner, she moved silently to the open porch and the stairway to the second floor.

On the steps Libby clung to the handrail, keeping to one side in the hope that the steps would not creak. At the top, the upper porch lay in shadows. Unable to see where she was, Libby felt her way around.

Paul was right. Two doors led into the house. Which door was the right one?

If I knock on the wrong door, I'll give everything away. I'll wreck all that Jordan wants to do. I'll spoil the way Paul covers up that he's working for the Underground Railroad.

Standing there, Libby felt cold with fright. *Even if I get the right door, there might be other women in Hattie's room. What if I do everything wrong? What if I fail?*

Unable to make up her mind, Libby moved into the deep shadows in a corner of the porch. As she started to pray, she remembered Jordan's words. *"Just because you done one thing wrong don't mean you is goin' to do everything wrong."*

His words gave Libby courage. Still praying, she decided to wait. Minutes later, one of the doors opened. In the darkness Libby could barely make out who it was. Serena carrying little Rose.

Without stirring, Libby waited until Serena reached the bottom of the steps. Then she rapped softly on the door.

When Jordan's mother opened it, Libby whispered, "I'm Jordan's friend." Slipping through the opening, Libby closed the door behind her.

From a table Hattie picked up the stub of a candle. Holding it up, she studied Libby's face. "You is Jordan's friend?"

In the light Libby saw the wonder in Hattie's deep brown eyes. But Libby also saw the questions. Quickly she told Hattie what had happened, then said, "Your son Zack is to be sold in the morning."

A soft moan escaped the woman's lips. A moan quickly silenced.

"If you want to take your family away tonight, the peddler will help you," Libby said.

"Jordan will be there?" Hattie asked.

Libby had to be honest. "Jordan was supposed to be here many hours ago. We don't know what's happened to him."

"All day long I been prayin' for him," Hattie said. "All day long I been feelin' uneasy."

"If you want to go now," Libby said, "Zack could be far away by morning."

As the candle sputtered, she again saw the fear in Hattie's face. But then Hattie straightened. Closing her eyes, she stood without moving in a way that reminded Libby of Jordan. Hattie's stillness grew long, and Libby knew she was praying.

When Jordan's mother opened her eyes, she spoke softly, but there was no doubt that she had made up her mind. "I ain't supposed to go," she said.

"Why?" Libby whispered.

"It ain't just leavin' here that counts," Hattie told her. "We needs to go miles and miles crost land, and swamps, and rivers. It ain't just anybody who can lead our people to freedom."

Hattie's brown eyes showed her anguish. "Long time ago the good Lord called my Jordan to lead our people out. If I goes now, he won't know where I is. If he ain't able to find me and Serena and

Zack and little Rose—if he worry about where we is, my Jordan will search till he gits caught."

Hattie drew a long trembling breath. "I is stayin' here till Jordan comes."

"You're sure?" Libby asked.

"I be sure."

Deep inside Libby felt even more afraid for Hattie. *If Jordan doesn't come—if Zack is sold in the morning—*

As though understanding Libby's thoughts, Jordan's mother spoke again. "I ain't goin' to tell Serena what you said. If Massa Weaver question her, she be unable to tell him anything."

"I'll leave before she comes back," Libby said quickly.

"I thanks you, Libby," Hattie said softly. "I be prayin' all night for my family."

When Libby slipped out on the porch, she heard soft steps on the stairway below. Quickly she stepped into the shadows. Still holding little Rose, Serena passed Libby, not two feet away.

In the wagon again, Libby could not sleep. Dread of what the morning might bring lay heavy upon her.

13

Jordan's Signal

I can't possibly make a drawing of the family, Libby told herself. Until now she had only tried sketches of individuals. She couldn't think of anything more difficult than doing a whole family and their house besides.

As frightening as that was, it seemed easy when compared to helping Jordan's family escape. During his years of slavery, Jordan had thought about countless ways to rescue his family. Since becoming a fugitive, Jordan had often talked with Caleb about what to do.

Now it seemed as if nothing was going to work. Frightening questions kept popping into Libby's mind. *What if Zack's new owner comes before Jordan gets here? And what if Jordan gets here and can't do anything?*

For the first time in her life, Libby hated the gray light before dawn. *Jordan's mother must dread the rising of the sun!*

Before daybreak Libby crawled down from the wagon. She and Paul walked to the big house together. When Libby went into the kitchen to get breakfast, she found Mrs. Weaver and Hattie already there.

Mrs. Weaver's eyes were red and puffy from crying. Yet her

"Good morning, Libby," sounded cheerful, as if nothing had happened.

Nearby, Hattie stood tall and straight with her hair short and curled close to her head. With sure hands she spooned up two bowls full of grits. Giving no hint that she had seen Libby during the night, Hattie acted as if it were an ordinary day.

Then Libby looked closer. Hattie's face was not peaceful, as Libby first thought. Instead, she wore the same blank look Libby had first seen in her son Jordan. That look hid every thought, whether joy or pain. It hid every attitude, even anger and fear. By now Libby knew that slaves used that look for protection—to hide feelings it would hurt them to show.

As Libby picked up the two bowls, Mrs. Weaver spoke to Hattie. "When we finish eating breakfast, I want you to pack a big basket of food. Take it down the road to Mrs. Lawrence. I hear she's doing poorly."

Halfway to the door Libby stopped and glanced back at Mrs. Weaver. *She doesn't want Hattie around when her son is sold*, Libby thought.

As though someone had kicked her in the stomach, Libby felt the pain. But Hattie's eyes held that same blank look. Not even a slumped shoulder gave away the pain in her mother's heart.

When Libby brought the two bowls of grits outside, she and Paul sat down on the kitchen steps. From there they could see what was happening behind the house.

Near one of the slave cabins, a skinny eight-year-old boy sat on the ground. Alone and shivering with the coolness of the morning, he ate his grits slowly, as if wanting to make them last.

Libby glanced toward Paul. "Zack?" Libby whispered.

"I think so," Paul answered softly.

Then Zack stood up. As if hating each step, he walked toward a shed for storing tools. With a hoe over his shoulder, Zack followed the older slaves to the cornfield behind the house.

Moments later the sun edged above the horizon, but darkness filled Libby's heart. With every passing moment her dread of what the day would bring grew stronger. As though matching her mood, clouds began building up beyond the woods on the far side of the field.

Standing up, Libby looked through the kitchen door. When she found no one inside, she told Paul what Mrs. Weaver had said.

"What if Jordan comes, and he can't even *find* his family?" Libby asked.

Paul shushed her, and Libby lowered her voice still more. But she still felt upset. "Zack one direction, Jordan's mother another, little Rose—" Libby broke off. "Where's little Rose?"

"In one of the slave cabins. The old woman you saw yesterday takes care of her during the day."

"What do we do?" Libby whispered.

"Pray."

Pray. As doubt crept into Libby's mind, she remembered Gran and Pa saying, *"God go with you, Libby."* She remembered Jordan's mother praying all night. And she thought about Jordan praying, *"We thanks you, Jesus, that when we is weak, you makes us strong."*

When I am weak, then am I strong? The words echoed in Libby's thoughts. *Maybe it's good to feel weak, so I let God help me.*

Unable to sit still any longer, Libby stood up. "Do you have a board I can use?" she asked Paul. "Something I can set up for an easel so I look like a real artist?"

As soon as Paul put together an easel, Libby carried it to the front of the house. Then she set her drawing paper in place.

Looking up at the house, Libby drew light, quick lines. After deciding where she wanted each person to be, she returned to the peddler's wagon. Paul was packing everything away, preparing to leave.

Just then Libby saw a farm wagon far down the road. "Maybe it's Caleb and Jordan!" Libby whispered.

A minute later she decided she was mistaken. The person who held the reins wore a straw hat pulled low over his eyes. The young man beside him wore a suit, white shirt, and a hat.

Still closing up shelves, Paul moved around to the other side of his wagon. When Libby followed him, the tall sides of the peddler's wagon stood between her and the house.

As Libby watched, the farm wagon drew closer. It had lower sides than the Stillwater wagon. In the back end Libby saw a large trunk and the cloth bags with handles that people called carpet-bags.

Then Libby realized there was something familiar about the people after all. While Jordan held the reins, Caleb leaned back as if he didn't have a care in the world. "It *is* Caleb and Jordan!" she whispered to Paul.

Libby wanted to shout, "They're really here!" Instead she quietly asked, "What if Zack's new owner comes right now? What do we do?"

Within a few minutes the horses reached the driveway. As they started the turn, a corner of the wagon tipped, leaned at a crazy angle, and dropped down. One of the wagon wheels rolled off into the field.

"Oh *no*!" Libby groaned. "What else can go wrong?"

As she and Paul watched, Caleb and Jordan climbed down to inspect the wheel. While Jordan rolled it toward the wagon, Caleb stalked up the driveway. In a suit and hat he looked at least three years older than he was.

When Libby moved forward to catch a better look, she realized that Mr. Weaver had come out on the front porch.

"Good morning," Caleb called to him, politely lifting his hat. "We're having a bit of trouble."

"I see that."

"My boy says he knows how to fix it," Caleb said. "The nut came off the wheel."

"I keep nuts on hand," Mr. Weaver answered. "Maybe I can help you out." Then he glanced toward Paul. "Come to think of it, my family and I are about to sit for a picture. The peddler will have exactly what you need."

When Caleb called to him, Jordan started up the long driveway. With bowed head and hunched shoulders Jordan shuffled as he walked.

"I say, hurry up!" Caleb called to him. "We haven't got all day!"

The shuffle and bowed head made Jordan seem helpless and weak. For an instant he stumbled, then caught his balance. Picking up his pace, he kept on.

By the time Jordan reached the peddler's wagon, Libby, Caleb, and Paul stood on the side away from the house. When Paul opened a drawer as though he was looking for a nut, Libby spoke quickly.

"Mr. Weaver has sold Zack," she told Jordan. "His new owner is coming this morning."

Jordan moaned. "He be comin' *this* morning?"

Libby nodded. "I heard Mrs. Weaver arguing with her husband."

Jordan's eyes blazed with anger. "Does Momma know?"

"I told her last night," Libby said.

"Then we leaves right now," Jordan answered.

"Right *now*?" Caleb asked. "It's broad daylight. If Zack is sold, maybe we can go where he is and steal him away tonight."

"Or maybe we can't," Jordan said. "Where's Zack now?" he asked Libby.

"In the field behind the house. I think Rose is in a cabin."

"My sister Serena?"

"We haven't seen her yet this morning," Libby said. "Probably in the house."

"Then we leaves now," Jordan said again.

"With a broken wagon?" Then Libby remembered. There was something that would make the rescue even more impossible. "I heard Mrs. Weaver tell your momma to take a basket of food to a neighbor."

"She did?" Jordan grinned as though he wanted to laugh out loud. "Then we is sure enough ready to go!"

"Jordan, are you certain about this?" This time it was Paul who warned him. All of them knew that most fugitives hid during the day and traveled at night.

Jordan's grin faded. His eyes were serious as he looked into the peddler's face. "Deep down here—" He thumped his chest. "And right here—" He tapped his forehead. "I know what the Lord be saying. He tells me, 'Go *now*!'"

"Then you tell us what you want us to do," Paul answered.

Before Jordan could say another word, Libby heard people talking on the porch. When she looked around the wagon, Mr. Weaver and Melanie were there, as well as a slave setting chairs on the lawn. Snatching up her pencils and paper, Libby hurried over.

When Mrs. Weaver came out, she carried Randolph. Glancing toward the road, she noticed the wagon. "What's wrong?" she asked her husband.

As he explained, Caleb and Jordan came around the peddler's wagon. When Caleb started toward the house, Jordan shuffled along several steps behind him.

Mrs. Weaver called back into the house. "Serena!"

A moment later Jordan's sister appeared. With her head bowed and her gaze on the ground, Serena stepped out on the porch.

"Get these men some water from the well," Mrs. Weaver told her.

As Serena turned, her gaze lifted. For one instant she glanced toward Jordan. In that moment glory filled her eyes. Then Serena's face went blank.

"If you wants water for the horses, the well's back here," she said and started around the house.

"I'll wait," Caleb told the Weavers. "My boy will take care of everything."

As Libby guided the family members into their places, Caleb leaned against one of the white pillars on the porch. For Mrs. Weaver Libby chose a chair in the center. Standing behind his wife, Mr. Weaver. Young Randolph in Mrs. Weaver's lap. Jonathan on the ground on the left. Melanie standing on the right.

At first Caleb's presence made Libby even more nervous. It was bad enough trying to do something she knew she couldn't do. But to pretend that nothing life-shaking was happening made it even worse.

Where do I begin? Libby didn't even know whether to work fast or slowly. *How much time does Jordan need?*

With Caleb standing behind the family, Libby could see him every time she looked up. *Oh, Caleb, don't watch me!* Libby felt uncomfortable enough as it was.

Then as she glanced toward Caleb, he lifted his hat and grinned. For all the world he looked like someone enjoying a pleasant morning. But to Libby his smile seemed to say something more—*You're doing okay.*

Raising her head, Libby tossed her long red hair. *All right, Caleb Whitney. You and Jordan are putting on a good act. God will help me too.*

As though she had drawn a family picture a hundred times before, Libby stood back, checking their positions. Yes, she had it right. Behind the family, the tall pillars on the front porch reached up to the second floor and the roof.

Because she had found it easy to draw Randolph, Libby started with him. She decided she would sketch only the face and shoulders of each person. If she put them close together, she could show the house in the background.

I can do this, Libby told herself. She felt sure it was God's power she was sensing.

But then she started to draw Jonathan. When Libby smiled at him, he scowled. He also had trouble sitting still.

I don't blame you, Jonathan, Libby wanted to say. *If it were my best friend being sold, I'd be upset too. I'm upset not even knowing Zack.*

While looking up at the family, then down at the easel, Libby kept an eye on Melanie. More than once the girl glanced back at Caleb as if trying to catch his attention.

As Libby started to draw Mrs. Weaver, Jordan shuffled back to the wagon. Her pencil moving swiftly, Libby sketched the outline of the woman's head, then filled in her face. Partway through, Libby felt glad she could hide the puffiness around Mrs. Weaver's eyes. Instead, Libby drew the warm, gentle look Mrs. Weaver had when she came to the peddler's wagon.

Soon, in the difficulty of what she was trying to do, Libby forgot even Caleb. *If I can just keep the family here long enough. If I can give Jordan the time he needs.*

When Mr. Weaver looked beyond Libby, she turned, wondering what was going on. Jordan was placing a jack under the axle of the wagon.

Libby had drawn Melanie's chin and eyebrows when she heard someone singing.

Singing? Instantly Libby grew still. How could Jordan sing at a time like this? But there it was. Libby recognized his voice.

Once again she stole a glance toward the end of the driveway. Kneeling on the ground, Jordan had set the wheel in place. But Libby clearly heard his words.

> *Steal away, steal away,*
> *steal away to Jesus!*

Inwardly Libby gasped at Jordan's daring. *Steal away? Sneak away?*

"Listen!" Mrs. Weaver held up her hand. "Caleb's boy is singing while he works."

Steal away, steal away home,
I ain't got long to stay here.

Behind the family gray clouds raced across the sky. Afraid to move, afraid that anything she might say would be wrong, Libby looked down at her easel and pretended to draw. "Listen for a signal," Paul had told Serena.

From far off, somewhere in the distance, Libby heard the roll of thunder. Jordan's voice grew stronger.

My Lord calls me,
He calls me by the thunder;
The trumpet sounds within-a my soul;
I ain't got long to stay here.

Then, as quietly as Jordan had begun, his voice faded away. When Libby dared look at Mrs. Weaver, tears stood in the woman's eyes.

"Isn't that beautiful?" she asked.

"Beautiful!" Her husband frowned. "Libby, let's hurry this up." Turning, Mr. Weaver shouted toward the house. "Serena!"

Moments later she appeared on the porch. "Yes, Massa." Serena's voice trembled, but her face gave no hint that she knew what was going on.

"Go and fetch your brother. Tell him to stop at the pump and wash up. Be sure he looks his best."

"Yes, Massa."

As Serena fled, Libby watched Mrs. Weaver. Her face white and still, she set her lips tightly, as though willing herself not to cry. But her arms tightened around young Randolph.

Libby started to shade in Melanie's eyes. When she glanced toward Paul, he had hitched his horses to his peddler's wagon. *So he's ready to leave at a moment's notice.*

Then from around the corner of the house came Jordan's mother. With Rose in one arm and the handle of a basket of food over the other, Hattie started down the driveway.

"Where's Hattie going?" Mr. Weaver asked.

"I told her to take food to the Lawrence family," Mrs. Weaver answered. "Mrs. Lawrence is doing poorly."

"Good thinking, Dorothy!" Mr. Weaver looked relieved. "I'm glad we're not going to have a big scene."

Again he turned to Libby. "I've got important business to tend to."

As Libby nodded, she glanced down. In horror she saw her drawing of Melanie's face. *I forgot to change her eyes. She looks the way she is!*

14

Bloodhounds!

$\mathcal{A}$s Libby's stomach tightened, her nervousness returned. She had no idea what to do to make Melanie look better. As though reflecting Libby's mood, the air felt heavy with the gathering storm. Then Jordan started singing again.

Steal away, steal away,
steal away to Jesus!
Steal away, steal away home,
I ain't got long to stay here.

The words calmed Libby enough to start drawing Mr. Weaver's face. From where he stood leaning against the pillar, Caleb straightened.

"It looks as if my boy has our wagon ready," he said. "I sincerely thank you for the help you've given us." With a polite lifting of his hat, Caleb started down the driveway.

Forgetting herself, Libby stared after him. The wagon was sitting at the right angle now. Jordan had turned the horses to face north, the direction from which they had come. Straw hat on his head, he sat on the high seat with the reins in his hands. The moment Caleb climbed up, the horses moved out.

"Libby, hurry along now," Mr. Weaver said. "I've got important business to deal with." Again he turned to the house. "Serena! Where is that girl?"

Moments after Mr. Weaver turned back to Libby, she saw Serena. In the field behind and to one side of the house Serena carried four wooden buckets.

Buckets? Libby wondered. As she filled in Mr. Weaver's eyes, her pencil broke. Libby snatched up another.

"Stop!" Mr. Weaver commanded. "This is nonsense, standing here like this. Libby, you don't know what you're doing!"

"How far are you, Libby?" Mrs. Weaver asked. "Please," she said to her husband. "This is important. I want a family picture."

As though she had not heard Mr. Weaver, Libby continued drawing. The next time she glanced up, she saw Zack carrying two of the buckets, Serena the other two. Side by side, they headed across the field toward the creek.

Curious now, Libby wondered what Serena had told the men in the field. Had she sent Zack on some unknown errand instead of back to the house? Beyond the open field, woods stretched off in the distance.

"Stop!" Mr. Weaver commanded again. "That's enough!"

Impatience written in every line of his face, he crossed the lawn to where Libby stood. When he looked down at her drawing, he drew back in anger. "That's supposed to be *me*? This is the most awful drawing I've ever seen!"

Melanie hurried forward to join her father. "Of course it's not you, Daddy."

Leaning close, Melanie stared at how Libby had drawn her. "That's not how I look!"

Melanie's creamy white skin flushed an angry red. "If I were an artist, I'd do great things to your red hair!"

Uh-oh! Libby thought. *If her father forgets how I look, she'll help him remember.*

Still holding Randolph, Mrs. Weaver started toward Libby. But Jonathan went in the opposite direction, disappearing around the corner of the house.

Just then Paul motioned to Libby as though saying, "Come."

But Mr. Weaver wasn't done yet. "I will *not* pay for such a terrible picture!"

When Mrs. Weaver reached the easel, she looked down, studying the drawing. Again Paul motioned to Libby. "Come!"

With one quick movement Libby snatched the paper from the easel. Mr. Weaver stretched out his hand, but Mrs. Weaver was quicker. Stepping in front of her husband, she took the drawing from Libby.

"I hope you will accept my bracelet as payment for this drawing also," she said.

Libby nodded. In all the times she had dreamed about being an artist, she had never imagined something this awful. Holding back her tears, she picked up her pencils and the easel. "Thank you for letting me try," she said. "Thank you for giving me your time."

As Libby hurried toward Paul, Mr. Weaver's words haunted her. But then, like a gentle whisper, there was something Libby knew. *Facing something hard isn't the same as failing. I succeeded in giving Jordan time!*

Near the wagon Mrs. Weaver caught up to Libby. "You will be a fine artist someday," she said. A smile tugged at the corner of her mouth. "That is, if you aren't so honest."

The moment Libby climbed up to the high seat, Paul called out, "Giddyup!" Libby waved and called goodbye, but Mrs. Weaver's smile was already gone. Pain filled her eyes.

Soon Paul's horses turned into the main road in the direction Jordan had taken. While still in view of the farmhouse, Paul kept his horses at their usual pace.

"Where is Jordan's family?" Libby asked.

"You'll see," Paul answered.

Instead, Libby saw Jonathan racing across the field toward the woods. In spite of his weight, he ran like a deer, bounding over the young corn.

"Look!" Libby told Paul. "Jonathan's headed this way."

The peddler's face was grim. "I hope we can trust him."

The moment the road passed into the woods, Paul looked back to be sure they couldn't be seen from the house. Then he slapped the reins across the backs of his horses. Instantly they picked up their pace.

Just then Libby heard the clip-clop of horses coming toward them on the road ahead. Soon two horses and a shiny new wagon came into view. As if anxious about more than the gathering storm, the driver urged his horses on.

Not far from the creek, Paul slowed his team to avoid meeting on the bridge. Without changing his speed, the other man kept coming. Before long, the two wagons met with Paul going north, the other man south.

"That's him," Paul said.

"Zack's new owner?" Libby asked.

"No doubt about it."

Twisting around to look back, Libby crawled onto her knees. Through the small square opening in the back of Paul's wagon, she watched the other wagon raise a cloud of dust, then disappear.

Soon after the peddler's wagon passed over the bridge, Libby saw Serena and Zack crawl out from under the heavy timbers. On the far side of the creek they climbed the bank of earth next to the bridge.

"There they are!" Libby exclaimed. "They used Jonathan's hiding place!"

"Whoa!" Paul called to his horses.

The minute the wagon stopped, Libby started to climb down, but Paul told her to wait. "There's more danger than you know."

Throwing the reins into Libby's hands, he grabbed a stout stick. "Hold the horses. Don't get down." Breaking into a run, Paul headed back along the road. "Zack! Serena!" he called.

As the children crossed the bridge, Jonathan came out of the trees on the far side of the creek. With one look Jonathan changed direction, heading toward the other children.

"Go, Zack!" he cried. "Hurry! Pa called out the dogs!"

Through the woods Libby heard their mournful baying—half bark and half howl. Running for their lives, Serena and Zack raced along the road toward Paul.

Jonathan ran after them, still shouting after Zack. "If you're free, you can go fishing!"

For only a moment Zack looked back. "When I catches that big fish, I is goin' to tell him about you!"

As Zack and Serena raced toward Paul's wagon, Jonathan

whirled around, running back the way he came. Closer and closer came the baying of the dogs. A chill ran down Libby's spine.

Then, where the trees thinned out, Libby saw the lead dog. At the head of the pack, he ran with his nose to the ground, picking up the scent. In a sharp voice Jonathan shouted a command.

Suddenly the bloodhound stopped. Again Jonathan gave the command. Reaching down, he grabbed the rope around the dog's neck.

When the other dogs started to catch up, Jonathan called to them. Though they looked confused, the dogs obeyed. As they gathered around the lead dog, their baying turned to whines.

In that instant Zack slowed down and glanced back. With Jonathan holding the lead dog, Zack waved to him. Only then did Libby recognize the bloodhound. Jonathan's pet!

Then Zack bounded on, following Serena. "Come with me," Paul said as they reached him. Moments later he shut them into the back of his wagon.

With one leap Paul climbed to the high front seat. Slapping the reins, he shouted at the horses. "Giddyup!"

Within a few minutes they reached the place where Paul and Libby had waited the afternoon before. Slowing the horses, Paul turned off the road into the woods. In the middle of the clearing, Caleb and Jordan were waiting for them.

The moment Paul stopped, Caleb opened the back door of the peddler's wagon. Zack and Serena jumped down and raced for the farm wagon. Between the large trunk and the carpetbags lay a number of blankets. Standing near the back end, Jordan helped Serena into the wagon.

As she crawled under the blankets, Zack looked up and recognized Jordan. Suddenly Zack threw himself at his brother. Jordan's arms closed around him. As if he would hug Zack forever, Jordan swung him off the ground. Spinning around and around, Jordan laughed as though playing a game.

But then he set Zack down. "You needs to hide."

When Zack disappeared beneath the blankets, Jordan glanced toward the woods.

"Your mother?" Libby asked.

Worry filled Jordan's dark eyes. "She ain't here yet."

Just then Hattie appeared between the trees. Her eyes wide with fear, she stood at the edge of the clearing. With little Rose in one arm and the handle of the basket over another, Hattie caught her breath.

Then her gaze rested upon Jordan. In that instant, all tiredness and fear fell away. With a step as light as a girl's, Hattie ran to her son.

Directly in front of Jordan, she stopped. Her gaze clung to his face, as if she could never see enough. With one swift movement she set down the basket and her child.

Reaching out, Hattie placed her hands one on either side of Jordan's face. A great sob rose from deep within. "My son! You has come back to me!"

When she opened her arms, Jordan stepped forward. In that instant a dog barked in the distance. Hattie jerked back as though remembering where she was.

"Hurry, Momma!" Jordan exclaimed. Lifting a blanket, he

waited as Hattie slipped Rose underneath. Then he held the blanket again as Hattie followed her child. With his family well hidden, Jordan raced to the front of the wagon, climbed up, and grabbed the reins.

"Jordan says to separate," Caleb said quickly to Paul. "He says you'll know when to find us."

Moments later the farm wagon passed onto the road. When Paul followed with his peddler's wagon, he let his horses plod along.

"Paul," Libby asked as they traveled at what seemed to be a snail's pace. "How did Jordan do that with the wagon? One minute it was broken, the next minute fixed."

Now that there was a moment to breathe, Paul looked as if he was enjoying himself. "Jordan's a mighty smart young man," he said. "He knows more about wagons than a lot of men twice his age."

Paul glanced back over his shoulder, and Libby turned to look behind them. So far no one followed.

"There's a nut on a wagon axle," Paul said. "A big nut, about three or four inches across. The nut holds the wheel on the axle."

Paul grinned. "But Jordan knows wagons, or he wouldn't know how to loosen the nut. If a wheel turns right, the nut is threaded right, so it tightens as the wheel rolls along. If a wheel turns left, the nut is threaded that way—again so it tightens as the wheel rolls. If you don't know which way to turn the nut, you can't get it off."

"But I didn't see Jordan stop and do anything," Libby said. "He and Caleb drove up right in front of Mr. Weaver and us. Suddenly, as they turned into the driveway—" Libby stopped to think about it.

"The wheel came off," Paul said. "But a short way back, probably just out of sight of the house, Jordan took off the nut. Then he drove the horses straight ahead, knowing that if the wagon didn't turn, the wheel would stay on. But the moment the wagon turned—"

Libby giggled. "The wheel fell off! All Jordan had to do was put it back on."

"And screw the nut the way it needs to go."

Again Paul glanced back. "Where did Jordan learn all this?" he asked as he looked forward again.

"Jordan says his daddy taught him. Jordan says he has value because of all he knows about horses."

"Jordan has value all right," Paul said. "Probably in more ways than we can begin to guess. He's a very gifted young man. Now that he's free, he's going to go far in life."

Soon Paul had another question. "Jordan's father?" he asked. "Where is he?"

"Sold away from the family," Libby said. "Jordan doesn't have any idea where he is."

"I was afraid you would tell me that," Paul answered. "I wonder if Jordan will ever see his father again."

Just then Libby heard the pounding hooves of horses coming up fast behind them. Paul's hands tightened on the reins.

15

The Fox River Outlaws

*B*efore long five men on horseback appeared at Paul's side of the wagon. As his spirited black mare danced around, Mr. Weaver told Paul to pull over.

"We're looking for two runaway slaves," he said. "A boy and a girl. The dogs lost their scent in the middle of the road, so they might have crawled into your wagon."

"That so?" Paul asked.

Just two runaways? Libby wondered. *So Mr. Weaver doesn't know about Hattie and little Rose. Or maybe he knows more than he's telling.*

"I'm going to check out your wagon," Mr. Weaver said as though he had no thought of asking permission. But Paul didn't ask him for a search warrant.

"If you're careful, you may look," he said instead. "I don't want any of my dishes broken."

As two men stood watch along the road, Mr. Weaver and the other two swung down from their horses. A short distance away their dogs waited. Panting and with tongues hanging out, they looked eager to be off on the chase.

They're bloodhounds, Libby reminded herself. Much as she wanted to push away her memory of the dogs chasing Zack and Serena, she couldn't. *They're bloodhounds trained to track down fugitive slaves.*

Paul climbed down so slowly that Libby found it hard to believe how fast he had run. Walking around to the end of the wagon, he opened the doors.

When one of the dogs leaped forward to sniff the back of the wagon, Paul warned Mr. Weaver. "If you let him scare my horses, I won't come to your farm again."

Mr. Weaver called off the dog, but two men climbed into the wagon instead. Turning, Libby watched them rummage around in the open area between where she sat and the back door.

Again Paul warned the men. "Careful now, careful. You won't gain anything by breaking my goods."

As though suspecting Paul's attempts to protect his property, Mr. Weaver glared at him. Whenever the men came to a box large enough for a child to hide in, they opened it. After checking even the drawers of the wagon, the men finally had to admit defeat.

"Now, gentlemen," Paul said when they finished searching. "Would you kindly set the boxes back the way they were? I don't want anything tossed around on these rough roads."

A cloud as angry as the gray sky spread across Mr. Weaver's face. Clearly he was anxious to be off. Just the same, Paul waited, and Mr. Weaver told the men to straighten out the mess.

As they pushed the boxes back into place, Libby watched Paul. Looking calm and patient, he waited as though he had no hurry to be off. *He's giving Jordan all the time he can*, Libby thought.

A large raindrop splatted on Libby's arm. A moment later more drops wet the dirt road, filling Libby with hope. *Maybe, just maybe—* A good rain would help Jordan and Caleb get away. But a minute later the rain stopped, and the clouds moved around them.

When all the boxes were in place, Mr. Weaver finally said, "If my slaves aren't with you, they're with that young man whose wheel rolled off. It won't be hard to find him."

From his spirited black mare, Mr. Weaver looked down at the peddler. "Good day, Paul. We can't be too careful, you know."

Paul seemed to agree. "You're right, Mr. Weaver. We can't be too careful."

"What do we do now?" Libby asked as the men and their dogs disappeared in the distance. She felt shaky just thinking about how close Serena and Zack had come to being caught.

"I'm going to let Caleb and Jordan find me," Paul said. "Now that I've been searched, it would be a good time for them to take my wagon."

In contrast to the way Libby felt, Paul looked as calm as if he faced narrow escapes every day of his life. *Maybe he does*, Libby thought.

They had driven an hour when she saw a farm wagon swing out of the woods into the road. "They're behind us, Paul," Libby said.

At the next place where he could leave the road, Paul turned the horses off between the trees. Caleb and Jordan followed him.

"Do you want my wagon?" Paul asked Jordan when the leaves of the trees hid all of them from the road. "We've already been searched. You and your family could ride inside."

To Libby's surprise Jordan looked uncertain. "I ain't sure," he said. "It seems like we is supposed to walk. But it don't make sense. It such a long way for Momma and Serena and little Rose."

Then, as if feeling he had no choice, Jordan nodded. "My family and I thanks you." As Jordan's family slipped into the back of the peddler's wagon, Paul stepped down from the front.

"Keep a sharp watch on the horses," he said as Caleb climbed up to the seat next to Libby. "Don't forget the Fox River outlaws. They're always looking to steal a good team and whatever else they can find. The closer you get to the Iowa border, the more apt you'll be to run into trouble."

Somewhere Caleb had changed his suit for an old coat and pants. Now Paul swept the black hat off his head and onto Caleb's.

Libby stared. Until Paul ran down the road she had thought of him as an old man. Without the hat, he seemed only a bit older than Pa. Not *really* old, but more the age of Caleb's grandmother.

With his blond hair covered and the old clothes, Caleb looked like a different person from the young man who stopped at the farm. "I'll leave your wagon at the next station," he told Paul, and Libby knew Caleb was talking about a home where the owners sheltered runaway slaves.

"If you get that far," Paul answered quietly. "God keep all of you."

His last farewell was to Libby. "Tell your pa he raised a mighty brave daughter."

As Caleb called "Giddyup!" to the horses, Libby caught his quick glance in her direction. But she could not meet his gaze. In spite of what Paul said, she didn't feel even one bit brave. Instead, she was scared about all that could still happen.

When they reached the edge of the woods, Caleb waited inside the line of trees until he was sure the road was clear. Soon the horses turned north and settled into a trot.

Although she wanted to ask at least one hundred questions, Libby found it hard to be with Caleb again. Their argument about the newspaper reporter had started the problem. But for Libby it was more. Caleb hadn't wanted her along. He knew how she had failed and didn't trust her to help Jordan's family.

At the farm this morning, Caleb seemed to encourage me, Libby tried to tell herself. Then she pushed the memory away. *That was just part of his act.*

Two weeks ago she would have liked being with Caleb. Now she felt awkward and uncomfortable. With her back as straight as an arrow, Libby stared ahead.

Out of the corner of her eye, she saw Caleb glance her way again. But Libby remained silent so long that Caleb finally asked, "Cat got your tongue?"

Only then did Libby know where to start. "Yesterday—last night—when you couldn't get to the farm. What happened?" As though she were still living that nightmare, Libby felt her dread during that time of waiting.

"Remember the Stillwater prisoner?" Caleb asked.

"How could I forget?" Yet so much had happened that even Sam McGrady seemed miles and years away.

"He followed us out of Keokuk. Three times we thought we had gotten away. Three times we saw him following us again. It was like he knew where we were going."

"That's why it took you so long?"

"We couldn't let him capture Jordan, and we couldn't let him follow us to the farm. We had to keep taking the long way around. There's something about a thief—"

Libby waited as Caleb thought about how to explain. At last he said, "A thief knows how to hide out. Maybe that made it easier for him to guess what we were doing to get away from him."

Caleb grinned at Libby. "Sam McGrady is a smart thief. But we're smarter."

Listening to Caleb, even Libby's dread of the prisoner fell away. She was just starting to feel better when Jordan leaned forward to talk in Caleb's ear.

"We needs to stop and find a hiding place."

When they came to a trail leading off the road, Caleb directed the horses into the woods. The wide dirt path wound through gently rolling hills. In the middle of a clearing they found the ruins of what appeared to be a log house that had burned down. To one side was a tin-roofed barn.

Jordan jumped out of the wagon to inspect the barn. Soon he returned and led Caleb around to the back. When Jordan pulled open a large double door, Caleb drove inside. Jordan closed the doors behind them.

They had come into the large open area where a farmer brought in a hay wagon. By standing on the wagon, a man could fork hay up into the loft on either side.

While Jordan stood watch, his family stayed inside the peddler's wagon. Caleb walked back to the road to made sure no wheel marks would give them away.

The trail is dry, Libby thought, feeling grateful that rain hadn't turned it into mud.

When Caleb returned, Jordan told his family that it was safe. Serena and Zack scrambled down from the back of the wagon. Hattie handed little Rose to Serena. As Jordan's mother climbed down, her hand rested on her younger son's shoulder.

"You is still with me, Zack!" The glory light shone in Hattie's eyes. "You is still with me!"

Glad to stretch their legs, Serena, Zack, and little Rose moved around in the large open area next to the wagon. For a time Libby stood watch, peering through a window on one end of the barn. At the other end, Caleb kept a lookout in a different direction.

When it came time for Libby to rest, she climbed a wooden ladder to the loft. Hattie and her younger children were already there. In the shadows along one wall they lay on a mound of hay, fast asleep.

Sinking down into another soft mound, Libby stared up at the wooden pegs holding the posts of the barn in place. Still thinking about all that had happened, she drifted off to sleep.

Libby's first waking thoughts were the sounds of spring. From a nearby pond peeped a chorus of frogs. Then Libby remembered she was hungry and thirsty.

When she looked over the edge of the loft, she saw Jordan try to pick up little Rose. Her eyes wide, Rose backed away from him.

Sitting down on the dirt floor of the barn, Jordan started talking to her. Instead of jabbering back, she hid behind her mother as if Jordan were a stranger.

Hattie tried to help the little girl understand. "Jordan be your brother, Rose, just like Zack be your brother."

But Rose would have nothing to do with Jordan. Each time he looked her way, she seemed afraid.

"She be good soon," Hattie told her son. "She were just too young when you was sold away. She don't remember you."

Soon Hattie took the cloth off the large basket of food and started feeding her children. As Libby climbed down from the loft, she felt curious about Hattie's escape.

"Do you think Mrs. Weaver knew she was helping you run away?" Libby asked.

"I 'spect she didn't want me to see my Zack being sold away," Hattie answered. Every now and then she glanced over to Zack and Jordan. Each time she looked at her sons, a smile lit her brown eyes.

As soon as Jordan finished eating, he started playing peek-a-boo with Rose. When the little girl giggled, her momma said, "Shush!" But Jordan looked pleased.

Taking out pieces of cloth, Hattie began dividing the food in her basket. Soon Hattie had bags for herself and Serena and Zack to carry on their back.

When Libby saw what Hattie was doing, she went to the wagon. From the food Paul had given her, she divided three portions—one for Caleb, another for Jordan, and a third for herself. Following Hattie's example, she too tied the cloth into bags.

On the very bottom of Hattie's large basket was a small cloth bag filled with something soft. When Hattie carefully packed it into a larger bag she could carry, it made Libby curious. But when Hattie said nothing, Libby felt afraid to ask.

By now the last rays of the western sun reached through a window. The light turned Libby's hair red-gold. To her surprise, Hattie noticed.

"Your hair is sure enough goin' to cause trouble," she warned.

Melanie, Libby thought. *Melanie talking to her pa.* But Libby pushed the thought away, not wanting to remember.

In the darkness before the moon came up, they gathered their few belongings and climbed into the wagon. With Libby on the front seat again, Caleb gave her the reins. Standing on the ground, he spoke into the closed-in part of the wagon.

"Ready?" he asked quietly.

"We is ready."

The sound of Jordan's voice startled Libby, for it came from only a foot or two behind her. Yet when Libby looked back, all was in darkness. She spotted no movement and heard no sound. Even little Rose was so quiet that Libby wouldn't have known she was there.

"We'll soon be close to the border between Iowa and Missouri," Caleb warned before he opened the barn doors, then closed them again behind the wagon. Walking without sound, he led the horses back along the winding trail. Before entering the road, he climbed up beside Libby and took the reins.

When the horses moved out, Libby stared straight ahead into the darkness. The rain that had threatened off and on all day had gone around them. Far above, the stars and moon shone brightly, lighting the road. As they passed a farm, the scent of pear blossoms reached Libby, but the beauty of spring was lost on her.

Several miles down the road, the horses rounded a sharp bend. Just ahead, a mid-sized tree lay across the road.

"Uh-oh!" Caleb pulled back on the reins.

As the wagon rolled to a stop, two men leaped out, one from either side of the road.

Then Libby saw it—the glint of metal. One rifle poked at Caleb's face. In the moonlight Libby stared down the barrel of another. When she saw the man at the other end, her teeth started to chatter.

16

You Owes Me!

*H*er mind numb, Libby didn't know if she was cold, or if it was fear she was feeling. Filled with panic, she tried to tell herself this wasn't happening. But she knew it was.

"Get down!" ordered a rough voice from Caleb's side.

Instantly Caleb turned slightly and whispered into the darkness behind him. "Go to Keosauqua, Iowa. The Pearson house."

As Caleb hesitated, the voice spoke again. "I said, get down, and get down now."

When Caleb reached out a hand, Libby realized her own hand was shaking. Caleb took it, speaking softly. "Come on this side. Do what I do. Don't try to be a hero."

The moment Libby stepped onto the ground, the man peered into her face. "Got a young'un here."

When Caleb didn't answer, it seemed to anger the outlaw. But the second man was already dragging the tree to one side of the road. Returning, he climbed up the far side of the wagon and sat down.

"C'mon, c'mon," he told the first outlaw.

To Libby's surprise the man's voice seemed familiar. Peering into the darkness, Libby tried to see him better. The outlaw's hat shadowed his face.

Still pointing the rifle at Libby and Caleb, the first outlaw backed away, then climbed up to the seat. As the driver slapped the reins, Caleb pulled Libby away from the wheel. A moment later, the peddler's wagon disappeared into the night.

"Well, there they go, over the border," Caleb muttered.

"Oh, Caleb," Libby wailed. "What shall we do?"

"You mean, what will *Jordan* do?" Caleb answered.

"Do you really think those outlaws will head for the border?" In spite of her terrible fear, it almost struck Libby funny. "That's where Jordan wants to go. But what a way to get there!"

Then the reality of what had happened struck Libby. Suddenly her knees felt wobbly. "That sweet little Rose in the hands of outlaws. And Serena and Zack and Jordan's mother! What will happen to them?"

"I don't know." Caleb sounded as upset as Libby felt.

"It's bad enough for those outlaws to stick guns in our faces!" she said. "But they're dragging Jordan and his family off to who knows where!"

Caleb took her thoughts a step farther. "Whoever they are, they must have read the wanted posters about Jordan. When they find out that he's with them, they'll remember such a big reward. Jordan's mother and the rest of his family will bring even more money."

Libby's dread grew. *Where's your favor, God?* she wanted to cry out. *Where's your protection?* After all the family had done to escape from the farm, the whole thing seemed terribly unfair.

Just thinking about it, tears welled up in Libby's eyes. Embarrassed now by her lack of courage, she tried to hold back her sobs. Instead, they broke loose, like water bursting from behind a dam.

"Hey, Libby—" Trying to comfort her, Caleb awkwardly patted her shoulder.

To Libby that seemed the final straw. Angry again, she jerked away.

"Libby, what's wrong?"

Instead of answering, Libby sobbed even harder. When Caleb

tried to lead her to the side of the road, she refused to move. Yet she could not stop weeping.

"Libby, what is *really* wrong?" Caleb asked. "Besides the outlaws, I mean."

When at last Libby drew a long ragged breath, her words tumbled out. "You didn't want me along. You thought you couldn't trust me to help Jordan's family. All this time I've been trying to prove that I could. But the worst of it is, you're right!"

Suddenly Caleb started laughing. Still standing in the middle of the road, Libby lifted her head, more offended by his laughter than by anything he could have said.

"How can you laugh at me in a time like this?"

Instantly Caleb grew serious. "Libby, just before the outlaws stopped us, I was thinking about the great job you've done. I don't know of another person in the whole world who could have stood in front of Mr. Weaver and kept drawing."

"Do you mean that, Caleb Whitney?" Libby felt sure he was teasing.

"I mean that, Libby. What's more, I'm proud of you."

"But you thought I wouldn't be up to such a hard trip. Now I know that I'm not! I'm scared half to death!"

"I'm scared too," Caleb said quietly. "I'm scared about Jordan and his family—"

"You don't show it."

"Nope. I can't show it."

Then Libby remembered Caleb's role as conductor in the Underground Railroad. During four long years he had trained himself to lead fugitives from one station—one hiding place—to the next. Often that meant Caleb needed to hide his feelings.

"And I'm scared about what might happen to you," Caleb went on.

"Me?" Lifting her head, Libby tossed her long hair.

"You," Caleb said again. "If something would happen to you, your pa—"

"So, it's not me you're worried about. It's my pa. It's what he would think!"

Caleb groaned. "It's more than that," he said as though trying again. "I'm sorry about our argument on the *Christina*."

"*Sorry?*" All the frustration Libby had felt burst from her lips. "After all this time, you're *sorry?*"

"Yes, I'm sorry. You were right. It was wrong the way I used the reporter to tease you. I should have played down the story about our accident. Instead, I made him *want* to write about it."

Caleb's apology upset Libby even more. "You let me suffer all this time!"

But then, standing in the middle of nowhere, Libby remembered why they were there. She remembered Jordan, and how he had forgiven even the slave trader Riggs. She remembered how it felt to fail and how it felt to be forgiven.

In the light of the moon, Libby saw the pain in Caleb's eyes. "I forgive you, Caleb," she said softly. "I forgive you for everything."

"Thanks, Libby." Caleb's voice was low, as if it was hard for him to admit his feelings. "I really care about what happens to *you.*"

Suddenly within Libby there was the feeling that a dam had burst. All of her walled-up anger, her bottled-up feelings, washed away. She straightened, standing tall.

As though Caleb understood that too, he reached out, took Libby's hand, and squeezed it.

When they again started walking down the road, Libby felt like a different person. Though her mind kept leaping to Jordan's family, there was no longer a high wall between her and Caleb. Though her dread of the outlaws remained, hope stirred in Libby's heart.

"Remember how Jordan prayed for love and protection and favor? Remember how he asked God to blind the eyes and shut the ears of people who would hurt us?"

"Or open the eyes and ears of people who would help," Caleb answered.

Libby felt shy trying to talk about her growing belief in God. Then she knew that was exactly what Caleb wanted her to do. *It's one of the things that makes him special*, Libby thought.

"Maybe we'll find wheel tracks and be able to follow Jordan," he said. "We can't keep up, but let's stay as close as we can."

Caleb set a good pace, and Libby half walked and half ran to keep up with him. They walked close to the edge of the road, ready to jump into the woods if someone came from either direction.

"It's strange," Libby said. "Jordan planned a midnight rescue for his family, but they had to leave during the day. Now it must be close to midnight, and we need another kind of rescue—a really big one."

A few miles down the road, Caleb suddenly stopped. When he turned to Libby, he only whispered a soft *Shhh!*

Not far ahead, the peddler's wagon had pulled over to the side of the road. When Caleb slipped into the woods, Libby followed. Moving forward as quietly as possible, they walked without making a sound. But when they drew close, they heard plenty of noise. Little Rose was crying at the top of her lungs. Hattie's efforts to quiet her seemed to have done no good.

One outlaw stood at the back of the wagon, guarding the door to keep anyone from getting away. A taller man stood at the front of the wagon, holding a rifle on Jordan. Libby and Caleb crept as close to him as they could. Kneeling down behind bushes at the side of the road, they peered between the branches.

The two outlaws were arguing. "They're not yours," said the man facing Jordan. "I get them!"

Again the voice seemed familiar to Libby. Squirming forward, she tried to see who he was, but could not.

"We're partners," the second outlaw answered. "Whatever we get, we divide half and half."

"Not this time. This boy is mine!"

"*Yours?*" The outlaw snorted. "Who do you think you are, telling me what to do?"

"I tracked this boy for a day and a night before he got away." The raspy voice was hard as nails.

Whoever the man was, Libby hadn't heard him speak often. *Once?* she wondered. *Twice? Who is he?*

"Okay," said the outlaw at the back of the wagon. "You can have the boy. But I get the rest. I'll take 'em south and get a good price."

"No, you won't!" The taller outlaw turned toward the other. "*All* of them are mine—all mine. I ain't splitting no reward with you."

That strange rasp. Libby struggled to remember. *The man who swam to the* Christina. *He said his name was Charlie Swenson. I wondered if he had a cold.*

Again she searched her memory, this time for a voice as hard as nails. *The man Jordan pulled from the water. The man who took one look and said, "It's you!"*

Libby shivered. "It's the prisoner," she whispered to Caleb. "Sam McGrady!"

Now that highly dangerous man faced Jordan with a rifle in his hands. Her terror growing, Libby remembered Caleb's warning to Jordan. *"Going back for your family may cost you your life."*

"Favor, God," Libby prayed silently. "Remember? Jordan asked you for favor."

Just then his voice broke into the argument between the outlaws. "I don't like the way you is talkin'," Jordan said. "You ain't got no right to me. You ain't got no right to my family."

"Who's talking about rights?" McGrady asked. "I'm going to collect the reward on your head!"

"No, you ain't," Jordan said. "You is an escaped prisoner."

"There ain't no one who's going to ask questions," McGrady answered. "All I do is bring you in and say, 'Here's the slave boy you been looking for.' And I collect big money."

"There ain't no money big enough to buy a man's life," Jordan said.

Sam McGrady's laugh filled the night air. But Jordan did not look away.

"I saved your life," he said.

"Ha!" Sam sneered. "I don't owe no slave boy nothing!"

"When you fell in that river, you got one chance." Jordan's voice was strong and steady. "If I hadn't grabbed you quick, you sure enough would be dead!"

"What's he talking about, Sam?" asked the outlaw at the end of the wagon.

McGrady shrugged. "Just a little slip I made on the way here."

"I is talkin' about what's right." Even in the dark, Libby saw the proud way Jordan lifted his head.

"What's *right*?" Sam asked. "I'm back with my friends, but you're a slave boy. Don't you ever forget!"

"There be somethin' I can't forget." Jordan made every word count. "I risked my life for you. There ain't no bigger sacrifice anybody can give. You owes me something!"

17

Dangerous Crossing

*I*n the silence that followed, not even Rose made a sound. Finally Sam McGrady spoke. "The boy pulled me from the river when my breath was knocked out."

"You fool!" exclaimed the other outlaw. "You don't owe him nothing!"

"Yes, I do." The rasp was still in McGrady's voice, but it sounded less hard. "The boy is right."

"Do you know what you're giving away? A two-hundred-dollar reward!"

"I would have been dead," McGrady answered.

"Well, I'm not such a fool!" the other outlaw answered. "I'm taking the woman and children. And I'm selling them to the highest bidder I find!"

"No, you ain't." Jordan's words shot out like bullets. "I expects you to let my people go."

When the silence stretched long, it was Sam McGrady who broke it. "His family goes with him," he said.

Without looking away from McGrady, Jordan called into the wagon. "Git down, Momma!"

Moving quickly, Jordan's family climbed down from the back of the wagon. Serena. Zack. Hattie. Then with her mother's help, little Rose. While they stood behind the wagon, the two outlaws climbed up to the high seat at the front. Sam McGrady took up the reins.

Jordan faced him. "Does you value your life?"

"I value my life." McGrady's voice was low but angry, as if he didn't want the other outlaw to hear.

"Then I wants you to do something else," Jordan said. "When you git across the border, leave the horses and wagon where honest folk can find 'em."

Instead of answering, Sam McGrady flicked the reins.

As the peddler's wagon moved away, Jordan and his family slipped into the bushes at the side of the road. Caleb waited until the wagon disappeared from sight, then hurried across the road after Jordan. Within a few minutes Caleb and Libby caught up to the family.

Caleb clapped Jordan on the back. "They're gone!" Caleb said. "But I wonder if McGrady will stick to his end of the bargain."

Jordan shook his head as if he too had his doubts. "We ain't goin' to take a chance on trustin' him."

Caleb agreed. "Sam might still want the whole reward for himself. If he does, he'll ditch the other outlaw and hunt for us again."

Just thinking about it, Libby felt afraid. But Jordan knew what he wanted to do. Instead of following a road, he cut across country, using the woods to hide from whoever might search for them. The rest of them followed single file with Zack and Serena close behind Jordan and his mother carrying little Rose next. Then came Libby with Caleb last.

They walked where there was no path, up steep hills, then down again. Libby's eyes grew used to the darkness, but she felt confused by the tall trees. Before long, she lost all sense of direction. But Jordan walked straight ahead as if he had been this way a thousand times before.

Feeling more bewildered all the time, Libby watched him. Again and again Jordan looked up to the night sky. When they stopped for a moment to rest, Libby asked how he knew the way.

"I is following the North Star." Jordan told her how to find it. "Look for the drinkin' gourd." He pointed up to the Big Dipper. The two stars on the side of the dipper away from the handle were pointer stars.

As they hurried on again, Libby thought about their enemies. *Mr. Weaver. Sam McGrady. The Fox River outlaws. Plus any slave catcher who might see or know about Jordan and his family.*

Libby had no doubt that slave catchers would patrol the border between Iowa and Missouri. More than once Caleb had told her that catchers watched the border in order to collect the reward offered for fugitives.

Whenever he had the choice, Jordan followed the steep, narrow valleys called ravines. Libby hoped the high banks on either side hid them from view. The muscles in her legs ached now, and she wondered if she could walk another step. Even worse, what Jordan was trying to do seemed impossible. How could he and his family ever find their way to safety and freedom?

Then like a whisper on the night wind, Libby remembered the promise. *"When I am weak, then am I strong."*

Looking up at the stars, Libby began to pray. "I am weak, Jesus. I'm tired and really scared. If I feel that way, what about Serena and Zack and little Rose? If they get caught, they'll lose their family—maybe even their lives.

"And what about Hattie—up all last night praying for her children? She's carried Rose mile after mile! But you promised, Jesus. You promised to help all of us. You promised that when we are weak, you will make us strong. Make us strong, Jesus! Make us strong!"

After a time, Libby remembered Caleb's whisper to Jordan. "What's at Keosauqua?" she asked.

"A crossing on the Des Moines River. An Underground Railroad station. I wanted Jordan to know about it in case the outlaws headed there."

"How do you learn about all these places?" Libby asked.

"I found out about Keosauqua because of something the town did. A fugitive slave and her children were hiding in a corn field." Caleb's glance took in Hattie and her children. "The woman had walked all the way from a plantation in the state of Mississippi. Though she had reached a free state, she was still afraid of slave catchers. She didn't dare ask for help, and she and her children were starving. When the people of Keosauqua learned that she was hiding in the field, they went to her and brought the family to safety."

Jordan had led their group for three or four hours when a cloud passed over the moon. Looking up, Libby saw other clouds darker than the night sky. One by one, they swept across the stars.

What will Jordan do? Libby wondered as her scared feelings came back. *Without the North Star, how will he know the way?*

But Jordan kept walking. Often he leaned forward to feel the bark of a tree. Whenever he found moss on the trunk, he moved on again, sure which way was north.

Before long, a drop of rain splashed against Libby's cheek. As she and the others came out of the woods to cross an open area, Libby felt more raindrops splat against her arms. Then came another and another. The rain that had threatened the day before was now here. Though Libby saw no lightning, thunder rumbled in the distance.

At first the rain came gently, offering welcome relief after the warmth of the day before. Then the gentle rain turned into soft pinpricks. Soon the wind drove the rain against Libby's face until it hurt.

By now Libby was angry. The harder it rained, the more upset she felt. Finally she cried out to God. "Jordan asked you to protect us! Where's your protection now?"

Holding Rose against her chest, Hattie crossed her arms over the child's head. Zack clutched Jordan's hand, taking three steps to Jordan's two. From all around came the sound of running water as creeks became torrents and new streams found their way down steep hillsides.

Grabbing Serena's hand, Libby bent her head against the wind, squinted her eyes against the rain, and kept on. Here in the open, the rain cut slantwise against them, but Jordan still kept on. As though he walked this way every day, he never slowed his pace. But Jordan had no path, no trail, no road. He just knew where to go.

Then, as suddenly as it came, the rain stopped. As Libby looked around, she saw water streaming down the side of Serena's face. Her thin sack dress hung about her knees, and she shivered with cold. Yet her bare feet followed her brother with sure, strong steps.

As the darkness of night changed to the gray light of dawn, Jordan stopped on a rise. Raising his arms, he lifted his hands toward heaven. "Thank you, Lord!" His quiet voice seemed to fill the earth. "Hallelujah!"

Only then did Libby understand what had happened. Only then did she remember that the rain had erased their tracks. No one needed to tell her, "That downpour washed away your scent for any bloodhound who might follow." No one needed to say, "You

aren't safe yet, but right now the bloodhounds can't follow Jordan's family."

Soon after Jordan went on again, they came to another thickly wooded area. There Jordan began to search for a place where they could rest during the day. He found it near the bottom of a tucked away ravine. "Git branches," he told all of them.

Together they hurried to find small branches blown down during the storm. In a hollow between two trees, Jordan and Caleb laid the branches so they appeared to have just fallen. Soon the branches and leaves offered a large enough shelter to hide the family.

While Libby watched in one direction, Caleb watched another. On her hands and knees, Jordan's mother crept into the hiding place. With little Rose safely in her arms, Hattie lay down to rest. Serena and Zack and Jordan crawled into the space beside her. Soon they were all asleep.

"Eat now," Caleb told Libby and the others in late afternoon. "We're close to the border. Right here the Des Moines River is a dividing line between Iowa and Missouri. We need to catch a ferry on its last run before dark."

And what if we don't? Libby wondered. She felt afraid to think about it.

But Serena was excited. "We is goin' into the Promised Land?" she asked.

"Iowa be a free state," Jordan told her. "But you won't be safe yet."

Hattie looked relieved to be this far, but Libby felt sure that she also knew the dangers ahead. Both Jordan and Caleb had told her about the slave catchers who roamed up and down the border to catch runaways.

As they finished eating, Hattie spoke to Libby. "I wants to thank you for comin' to my room and warnin' me about Zack." Whenever Hattie turned toward her younger son, a glad light shone in her eyes. Then her gaze rested on Libby's hair.

"When I was prayin', the Lord gave me a warnin' about you. Your hair be mighty pretty, Libby, but if we ain't careful, it goin' to get us in trouble."

"People notice my hair, don't they?" Libby remembered Melanie's anger. *If Mr. Weaver doesn't remember how I look, Melanie will tell him.*

"Does you have a sun bonnet with you?" Hattie asked.

When Libby pulled it out of the bag she carried on her back, Jordan's mother told her, "Then I got what you need." Hattie opened the small bag Libby had noticed before.

Libby started to giggle. "Is it flour?" she asked. "That will make my hair look dull and lifeless!"

Hattie smiled. "You'll look as harmless as a baby kitten."

Sweeping her long hair up and away from her face, Libby tied it in a knot. Hattie sprinkled the flour over Libby's head and worked it into her hair. Then Hattie tucked the leftover strands inside the back of Libby's collar.

"You is goin' to be full of flour, child," Hattie warned as Libby put on her bonnet. "But if we lets your hair swing free, all the flour might ride out."

When they started walking again, Jordan kept looking at the sky. As the sun dipped lower and lower in the west, he picked up his pace.

"What if we don't make the ferry on time?" Libby asked Caleb as they hurried along.

"We'd have to wait till morning." Clearly Caleb didn't like that idea. "Worst of all, we'd have to cross the river in daylight."

Libby glanced around. Here in the deep woods, it would soon be dark. Since their escape from the farm, the woods had given shelter to Jordan's family. But those same hills and woods offered all kinds of hideaways for outlaws.

"It's a bad spot," Caleb said as though hearing Libby's thoughts. "The Fox River outlaws have seven crossings on the Des Moines River and four on the Mississippi. When they commit a crime in Missouri, they use the crossings to escape to Iowa and Illinois. There's a good chance we'll find a thief somewhere around here."

"Or have him find us." Libby dreaded the idea. "It's no wonder you had trouble getting rid of Sam McGrady on the way down. He must have been going close to where you wanted to be."

"And I bet he knows this country like the back of his hand," Caleb said.

When they came to the edge of the woods, Jordan's family had their first look at the Des Moines River. Though both Serena and Zack knew the danger of speaking aloud, they gazed across the river with excitement in their faces.

But Caleb and Jordan looked upset. Up and down the river, for as far as Libby could see, there was no ferry.

"Which way does we go?" Jordan whispered.

Caleb shook his head. They had come out at the river, but at a different place than planned. Staying within the line of trees, Caleb stared at the broad, deep waters. Usually calm, he seemed more nervous by the moment.

"You go one direction, and I'll go another," he whispered to Jordan. Whoever found the ferry would call like an owl.

Every minute we stay here, the more chance we have of being found, Libby thought.

Searching for a better hiding place, Hattie moved her family farther back into the woods. Libby followed them, but as time grew long, she crept back toward the river where she could see the sun. Already it had dropped behind the trees in the west. With growing dread Libby watched the light sink lower and lower.

Then an owl hooted from upstream. From downstream Caleb answered with another hoot.

We'll make it! Libby thought as she looked in the direction Jordan had gone. If his family followed the flat, pebbly ground close to the river, they would make better time than in the woods. But as Libby started back to them, she glanced downstream. Just then a man on horseback rode out of the woods.

Afraid again, Libby stepped behind a tree to watch. The man gazed at the water as if wondering about a way across. But Libby had no time to waste. Avoiding sticks that would snap and break, she hurried deeper into the woods.

Soon Libby met Jordan's mother. She too had heard the owl and knew what it meant. As Hattie led her family upstream, Libby fell in behind them. Again and again she looked back over her shoulder.

As they walked, the light faded and the woods grew dark. Soon even the gray twilight that followed sundown would not help them. But just as Libby was ready to give up, Jordan found them.

"Where's Caleb?" he whispered.

Libby explained that she had seen a man between them and Caleb. "You better keep going," she said.

"And leave Caleb?"

"He would want you to," Libby said. "If you don't, all that you've tried to do might be lost."

Still Jordan did not want to go on.

"Maybe he'll catch up," Libby said.

Turning, Jordan started back upstream with his family walking close behind him. In the last gray light, they reached the ferry. Already the owner was loosening one of the ropes.

As the others stayed inside the line of trees, Libby ran forward. "Seven passengers," she said.

When the man named his price, Libby dug down into the bag she carried. Suddenly she realized that she had no money!

Fumbling around, Libby searched her bag for something to sell. Drawings? No. She didn't have any more. When she found the bracelet Mrs. Weaver had given her, Libby held it up.

But the owner of the ferry shook his head. "I ain't got no use for the likes of that. I got a family to feed." Turning his back on Libby, he walked over to another post and untied the second rope.

Palms up, as though asking what to do, Libby looked toward the woods. In that moment Jordan stepped out, followed by his family. As they hurried onto the ferry, Jordan took a coin from his pocket. The man stared up into his face, bit the coin, then nodded.

"I is paying for my friend too," Jordan said.

"It's enough," the man answered.

Just then Caleb raced out of the woods. As he leaped onto the ferry, the owner pushed off. They were halfway across the river before Caleb caught his breath.

As the twilight faded into darkness, Libby stared at Jordan. "Where did you ever get enough money to pay for all of us?"

Jordan straightened, wearing the proud look that reminded Libby of royalty. "Your pa been paying me for my work. When he gives me money, he says, 'Jordan, it be good havin' your help. You earned this.'"

Jordan turned toward his mother. "I been savin' the money for my family."

As tears welled up in Libby's eyes, she glanced toward Caleb.

To her great surprise he too was crying.

As the ferry drew close to the Iowa side of the river, Caleb spoke in a low voice. "Just do what I do," he told Jordan and his family. "And do it as fast as you can."

The moment the ferry touched land, Caleb was off. Like shadows in the night, Jordan's family followed, their bare feet making no sound. They had barely reached a hiding place when Libby heard noise from the other side of the bushes.

Crouching down, she and the others waited as lanterns swung back and forth. Then the lanterns moved away, down to where the ferry had tied up.

From across the river Libby heard the mournful baying of bloodhounds. *So! Mr. Weaver guessed where we'd come, even if his dogs didn't track us.*

With their half howl, half bark, the baying dogs filled the night with fear. Waiting in the darkness, Libby shivered.

18

The Secret Stairway

*H*alf standing, half crouched, Caleb started to run. When he reached the nearby woods, the rest of them were close behind.

For some time they walked without speaking, going deeper and deeper into the woods. They followed a path, Libby knew, but an unmarked path most people wouldn't see. Caleb was back in the area he knew well from his work with the Underground Railroad.

When they came to a barn where horses were harnessed and ready, Libby wasn't surprised. No one was around, but Caleb seemed used to being here. As Jordan and his family crawled under the hay in the back of the wagon, Libby took her place on the front seat. Caleb led the horses out and closed the door behind him.

The moment Caleb sat down beside Libby, he flicked the reins and the horses moved out at a steady trot. They had traveled only a few miles when a group of men rode out of the woods into the road.

"We're looking for runaway slaves," one of them said. "They told us to find a girl with red hair."

With a suspicious glare, a man held a lantern toward Libby. The light fell across her face.

As her hands started shaking, Libby tightened her fists. Keeping her hands in her lap, she forced herself to smile. "To set your mind at rest, you might like to see my hair," she said.

Telling herself that her fingers could not shake, Libby untied the strings of her bonnet. Carefully she raised it to show the hair that was now a dull, lifeless color.

"You see?" Libby asked, her voice still sweet.

In the glow of the lantern, the man stared at Libby's hair, then backed away. "Thank you kindly, miss," he said. "We're keeping the roads safe for you tonight."

As Caleb called "Giddyup!" to the horses, they moved out again. When Caleb finally looked at Libby, she saw his grin. Only then did Libby breathe deeply again.

About twelve miles down the road, the horses turned into a farm. As though they knew exactly where they were going, the horses stopped in front of the wide doors of a barn. Caleb jumped down to open them.

Once inside, he again closed the door. "It's okay," he said softly, and Jordan and Zack wiggled out from under the hay.

Together the three boys worked quickly to put the horses in stalls and rub them down. As they hitched up a fresh team of horses, another boy entered the barn.

"I'll leave them at the usual place," Caleb whispered to him.

As soon as Jordan and Zack again took their place under the hay, the boy opened the door. The moment the fresh team of horses stepped out, the door closed on well-oiled hinges.

When they were well away from the farm, Libby looked at Caleb. "I'm awfully glad you made it to the ferry," she said.

"Me too." Caleb's grin showed his relief. "Jordan could have taken you through the woods, but he wouldn't know the first station. From there someone would have taken you on. But it might have been hard getting that far."

Libby wasn't sure how many miles they had traveled from the ferry—twenty-five, twenty-six, or perhaps more. She only knew that it had to be about one o'clock in the morning when Caleb turned and spoke softly toward the back of the wagon.

"We'll be crossing the Skunk River," he said. "There's a ford here—stones put down like a road on the river bottom. The water shouldn't be more than three feet deep. But if it's higher—"

"We is ready" came Jordan's quiet voice.

At a worn-down place in the bank, the horses eased into the river, as though used to the crossing. Soon the water rose around their knees, then sloshed against their bellies. On the far side of the river, the horses plodded up the bank. When they reached the road again, they picked up speed.

"We're close, aren't we?" Libby asked as she watched them. No doubt about it, the horses knew there was feed and water not far away.

Twisting around, Caleb peered back in the darkness. "I don't like it," he said. "I feel uneasy, as if someone is watching me. But that has to be crazy. I've haven't seen anyone since those men near the Des Moines River."

"Where are we?" Libby asked.

"Augusta, Iowa."

"Could the horses keep going if we didn't stop?" Libby asked.

"If they had to, they could, but they need a rest," Caleb said. "And if there's someone behind us, we need to get rid of him somehow."

As the horses started up a long steep hill, Caleb again looked back. "Strange," he said. "I just can't explain it. But I've worked with the Railroad long enough to pay attention when I think something isn't quite right."

"Can you tell me where we're going?" Libby knew that "passengers"—runaway slaves—might go in and out of a station without ever knowing the names of the people who helped them.

Now Caleb surprised Libby by telling her about Dr. Edwin James.

"He's an explorer and a scientist," Caleb said. "On an expedition to Colorado with Major Long, Dr. James discovered plants and trees no one had named before. He was an army doctor too, and the first white man to climb Pikes Peak. For a while the mountain was named James Peak after him."

As Libby listened to the pride in Caleb's voice, she guessed the doctor was one of his heroes.

"But there's more," Caleb went on. "Dr. James translated the New Testament into the Chippewa language."

"And Dr. James must be part of the Underground Railroad," Libby said.

"Yup. A well-known part. That's why I can tell you about him. A few years back he was caught taking a fugitive named Dick across the Mississippi River. The slave catchers forced Dr. James back to Burlington, and Dick was thrown into jail. The courtroom has never been as full as it was the day of that trial in Burlington. The judge challenged the fugitive slave laws and set Dick free."

Caleb grinned his delight at telling the story. "A great shout went up in the courtroom. Those who hadn't been able to get inside cheered till the whole town echoed. A thousand men walked with Dr. James and Dick down to the river. There they cheered again while Dick started across on his way to freedom."

As they came into view of a small stone building, Caleb spoke quickly. "This chapel is on Dr. James's property. He has church here every Sunday. I'll leave all of you while I find him. If it's safe, he'll come get you, and I'll take care of the horses."

The minute they stopped Caleb gave Libby the reins and jumped down to check the little church. In a moment he returned and spoke softly to Jordan's family. As Caleb stood watch, they wiggled out from under the hay and slipped into the chapel.

The inside of the small building was dark, but a shaft of moonlight shone through one window. With Rose sleeping in her arms, Jordan's mother dropped down on a bench and rocked back and forth.

Jordan settled himself on another bench. Facing the door, he waited, alert and ready for danger. When Zack sat down on one side of him and Serena on another, Jordan's face softened.

Before long Libby heard a muffled sound outside the chapel. As the sound moved closer, she knew what it was—small stones rolling down a steep hillside. When Jordan leaped to his feet, Libby raced to a window.

Though she could see no one in the darkness, Libby again heard the sound. Muffled but distinct it came, as though someone stopped to listen, then walked on.

When the footsteps stopped once more, this time just outside the chapel, Jordan stepped behind the door. As it swung open, he waited while a man entered.

As the door closed again, the man turned toward Jordan's dark shape. "I'm Dr. James," he said as if he expected Jordan to be there. "Don't be afraid. Caleb asked me to come for you."

Slowly, as though not wanting to frighten anyone, the doctor moved toward the window. When the moonlight fell across his face, he asked, "Did anyone follow you?"

"There be slave catchers after us," Jordan said.

"And maybe an escaped prisoner," Libby added.

"And a man who thinks we is his property," Hattie said.

"I see," said Dr. James. "You are certainly well liked. Then come quickly."

Dr. James opened the door, looked around, then led them outside. The chapel lay at the bottom of a wooded ravine. As they hurried up the narrow valley between steep hills, Dr. James walked tall and erect, like a person used to army life.

When he brought them into his house, Libby saw heavy curtains drawn across the windows. In the living room a huge fireplace nearly filled the wall opposite the door. As the red coals sent forth welcome heat, Libby and the others gathered around. By the light of the lamp, Libby saw kindness in the doctor's eyes. But he warned them.

"You can't stay this close to the front door. Ever since I was caught with a fugitive, slave catchers have watched my house day and night. Someone might come with a search warrant."

On either side of the fireplace were closet doors. When Dr. James opened one of them, it looked like the usual closet. Then he showed Libby the latch for a hidden trapdoor. The door in the wall opened onto a landing with a secret stairway leading both up and down.

"If someone comes to the door, you'll have to listen," Dr. James said. "If all is going well, you can stand on the stairs and be safe. But if the child starts to cry—"

"What does we do?" Hattie asked quickly, no doubt remembering how Rose had cried in the peddler's wagon.

"If the slave catchers go upstairs to hunt for you, go down in the basement. If you hear them walk down to the basement, creep upstairs. Even the walls can talk."

The doctor's housekeeper came then, bringing bread and cheese. "If you stay long enough, I'll have more," she told them.

"Something to warm up your insides. But don't leave even a crumb in the closet. It's the first place slave catchers look."

They were still eating when Caleb came in. As he wolfed down a sandwich, footsteps sounded outside the house.

"Hurry!" Dr. James pushed them toward the secret hiding place. "Get in the stairway and close the trapdoor."

Inside the closet Libby fumbled with the latch to the trapdoor. Caleb snatched up a candle and followed her. Reaching forward, he pressed the latch, and the trapdoor opened. When Jordan followed Caleb, Hattie shoved Serena and Zack toward him.

As Libby started up the secret stairway, she looked back into the living room. Little Rose stood next to the window. When her mother raced to get her, the little girl pushed aside the heavy curtain to look out.

Just then someone pounded on the front door. Libby's heart leaped into her throat.

"Get moving," Caleb said, but Libby was watching Rose.

Snatching up her child, Hattie raced for the closet. When Dr. James closed the door behind her, Jordan reached for his little sister. "Follow Caleb," he told Serena and Zack, and the two slipped past him.

"Hurry!" Jordan told his mother. Pulling her onto the landing, he closed the trap door leading to the closet.

As the latch clicked into place, Libby fled up the stairs. Through the walls, she heard the pounding on the outside door. Slow footsteps crossed the wooden floor, as if Dr. James was giving them all the time he could.

Remembering the doctor's warning about noise, Libby stopped on the second-floor landing. Behind her, the others waited. As Caleb held up the candle, Libby saw the stone wall of the chimney on one side of the secret stairway. Opposite the chimney, the wall was wood with openings into other parts of the house. In the light of the candle, Libby's shadow fell across the wall.

Walking on tiptoe, she grabbed the handrail and climbed another step, then another. Each time she moved, her shadow moved with her. As Caleb and the others followed Libby upward, their shadows flickered and danced in the candlelight.

From below, Libby heard voices. Listening, she tried to figure out how many men there were. "We're after some runaway slaves," one of them said.

"You'll find no slaves in this house," Dr. James answered, and Libby knew that like the Quakers he too believed in honesty, yet in the freedom of every individual.

"We'll have a look around," a second man answered.

"Not without a search warrant." The doctor's voice was firm.

"Here's your warrant." That was the third voice.

Barely breathing, Libby waited. When she heard no sound, she knew that Dr. James must be reading a paper.

In that moment little Rose whimpered.

"Hush, baby," her mother whispered. But Rose looked up at the dancing shadows and whimpered again.

"Move!" Jordan whispered, and Libby again started upward.

Her feet flying without sound, she reached the landing for the attic. Looking back, she saw Caleb, Serena, Zack, and Jordan fleeing up the steps. Last of all came Hattie with the child's head against her chest. As they passed the second-floor landing, Rose let out a wail.

Frantic with haste, Libby fumbled with the latch to the attic door. By the time she found it, Rose was sobbing as if her heart would break.

The minute Libby opened the trapdoor, she stepped into a closet. There she opened another door into a large attic room.

Still holding the candle, Caleb lit the way for the others. In the attic a window was open, and the current of air caught the flame. When Caleb gave Libby the candle, she cupped her hand around it.

Just then Hattie moved into the room. Rocking back and forth, she crooned softly to Rose. For the moment the little girl was quiet.

Peering around the attic, Libby tried to see into the shadows. *The main stairway. Where is it?*

Then she knew by the sound. Someone was coming up, no doubt taking the steps two at a time.

Libby raced for the closet and the secret stairway. As Serena and Zack, then Hattie followed, Caleb stayed behind to help Jordan close the doors.

In that moment Libby felt a current of air sweep down the steps. An instant later the candle flickered out.

19

Betrayed?

$\mathcal{S}$uddenly Rose shrieked. Close behind Libby, Serena gasped. Reaching back, Libby felt for Serena's hand, then grabbed it.

"Hang on," Libby whispered to Serena, then started down the stairway. With her other hand on the railing, Libby felt her way in the dark, doing her best to hurry.

Behind Libby, Serena's bare feet made no sound. Zack followed Serena, again without sound. Behind them Libby heard only a slight movement now and then.

When Libby reached the second-floor landing, she paused. Rose was quiet now, for the moment at least. From the other side of the wall next to her, Libby heard a voice. As clearly as if the man were on the stairway with them, he spoke with a rasp in his voice.

"No one here," he said.

The escaped prisoner, Sam McGrady!

Hearing him, Libby felt sick. *So you came back and managed to find us. Jordan saved your life, but you betrayed him!*

A moment later, heavy boots tromped off. Hardly daring to breathe, Libby heard footsteps on the main stairway. Then the steps moved still farther away, as if the men were going down to the basement.

For a time Libby heard the rumble of far-off voices. Then the men drew closer again. Whoever they were, the men were angry.

Soon the sound of their voices came from the living room. "We'll be back with more men," one of them said. "And some of us will watch you every minute till they come."

When the outside door slammed, it echoed up the secret stairway.

Even when Libby believed everyone was gone, she did not dare move. Finally Dr. James opened the trapdoor on the main floor and called to them.

"Follow the stairs down to the basement," he said. "We'll give you more food there."

In the basement Hattie sank down on a chair. As though exhausted with trying to keep Rose quiet, she rocked back and forth. But a tear slid down Hattie's cheek.

"I is sorry," she told Dr. James when he entered the room. "I done put you in danger."

"We can't expect a child not to cry," he answered. Again Libby heard the kindness in his voice.

As the housekeeper brought bowls of soup, Libby looked up in surprise.

"I can cook even if men are searching the house," the housekeeper said. "I just keep a pot simmering on the back of the stove."

"For the moment you're safe," Dr. James told them as he encouraged them to eat. "But I have no doubt that they'll be back with more men—so many men that it will be impossible to hide any noise."

"Is there any time when there's no one watching you?" Caleb stood at one side of a basement window. Through the narrow gap between the window and the heavy drape, he looked out.

"There's only one time when they seem to let down their guard," Dr. James said.

"At daybreak?" Caleb asked.

Dr. James nodded. "They watch all night, thinking we'll use the hours of darkness. Yes, daybreak is the most hopeful time."

"Then that be when we go," Jordan said.

The doctor smiled. "Your time is almost here."

As Caleb moved away from the window, he, Jordan, and the

doctor sat down together. When they started to make plans, Libby joined them.

"There's something we haven't counted on," she said. "When we were in the secret stairway I heard a voice right next to me. It was the escaped prisoner—Sam McGrady!"

"So that's why I felt uneasy when we crossed the Skunk River!" Caleb exclaimed. "Did the other men look like slave catchers?" he asked Dr. James.

"Two of them. The third man was well dressed. And the fourth man—the one with the raspy voice—had very short hair."

Jordan moaned. "That be the prisoner all right. I was hopin' he changed for the better!"

"Remember what you said?" Libby asked Caleb. "That it's harder to hide from a thief?"

Feeling as though she could not sit still, Libby moved over to the window. She too looked through the narrow opening between the drape and window. The light of the new day would soon break upon them. According to what most fugitives did, it was exactly the wrong time to leave. Yet they had no choice.

Libby tried to push aside her dread. *Jordan has tried so hard. We're only about seven miles from Burlington and the* Christina. *What if the escaped prisoner wrecks everything now?*

Even the possibility of that happening scared Libby right down to her toes. Then she remembered. *At first I thought I could do anything I tried. Instead, I made a mess of everything. But when I let God help me, that's when things changed.*

Turning, Libby faced Jordan. "Do you remember what you prayed before we left the *Christina*? That God would blind the eyes and shut the ears of the people who would hurt us? And that He would open the eyes and ears of the people He wants to help us?"

This time it was Libby who offered the prayer. When she started, her voice trembled. Then as she thought about God and not what the others would think, her voice grew strong. As she finished praying, Jordan and Hattie joined her with their own Amens.

"I didn't put the horses in the barn," Caleb explained when it was time to go. "They're in a shelter in the woods about half a mile away."

As they left, Dr. James stood by the door. "God go with you," he said to Caleb, Jordan, and Zack, then to Hattie, Serena, little Rose, and Libby.

"God go with *you!*" Libby said as she too passed out the door. *From Gran, Pa, and now Dr. James. God, go with us!*

One by one they followed Caleb. In single file, with Libby walking last, they crossed the yard to the edge of the woods. As Libby slipped between the trees, she glanced back along the side of the house.

Just then a man came over the edge of the hill. As he looked at Libby, he stopped dead in his tracks. Their gaze met as it had that morning in Prescott.

Then, as Mr. Weaver came over the hill, the escaped prisoner suddenly turned, taking Mr. Weaver with him. In the next moment both men disappeared behind the hill.

Whirling around, Libby broke into a run. "Hurry!' she whispered as she passed the others to reach Jordan. "Hurry!" she warned as the family slipped back under the hay. "Hurry!" she told Caleb as he leaped up to the high seat.

Only when they were well on the road to Burlington did Libby explain. "Sam McGrady saw us, but he turned the other way. He took Mr. Weaver with him."

Clearly puzzled, Caleb shook his head. "I don't understand," he said. "I don't understand at all. Why didn't McGrady stop us right then?"

When they entered Burlington the streets were still empty with the quiet of early morning. Caleb stopped the horses near the back door of a church. To Libby the building looked familiar, even from that side.

"The doors are open all the time," Caleb told her. "Wait inside. I'll be with you soon."

One by one Jordan and his family slipped from beneath the hay into the church. The minute Caleb returned he led them through the basement. On the front side of the church, out beyond an opening in the foundation, was a secret room.

As though Caleb had been there often, he closed the door behind Jordan's family, then lit a candle. From that candle Caleb lit another, and yet another, as though he wanted to celebrate.

It's home to Caleb, Libby thought. In that moment she knew where they were. *The First Congregational Church. Where Rev. Salter is pastor.*

Libby remembered the courageous man from her first trip to Burlington.

The hiding place seemed to be well used. Along one wall were jars of water and bowls of food. From a neatly folded pile, Caleb gave out blankets for the family to sit or lie down.

When Libby looked around the circle, she wanted to reach out to Serena. *Will we have time to become friends?* Libby wondered. Or would Serena be like other fugitives, passing on to the next station almost at once?

And Jordan, Zack, Hattie, and little Rose? What will happen to them?

Then as Libby's gaze rested on Caleb, he looked at her and grinned. *He's my friend again,* Libby thought with gladness of heart. *My very best friend.*

"Your pa isn't here yet," he said. "But he will be. By nightfall he and the *Christina* will be waiting for us."

As they waited throughout the day, Libby watched Jordan come to know his sisters and brother again. Here little Rose could play peek-a-boo and giggle at Jordan's games. Here Serena could put her hand within his. Here Zack could openly look up to the big brother he admired. And here Hattie freely gazed upon her family with the glory light in her eyes.

They're a never-give-up family, Libby thought. *They're a family that stays together even when it's difficult.*

After many hours in the secret room, Libby heard several quick knocks on the door. As if the raps were a signal, Caleb leaped up. Slowly he opened the door, looked out, then stepped into the hallway to talk to someone.

"We can go now," Caleb said when he came back. "Just walk like you're not afraid, as though you don't have anything to hide. But do what I do."

When they slipped out the front door of the church, Caleb led them. Jordan stood tall, wearing his proud look again. His family followed as if they walked this street most any day of the week. Yet they stayed within the shadows of the buildings on their right.

Two or three blocks away, Caleb brought them to Hawk-eye Creek. Crouching low, Jordan and his family followed the stream, hugging the shadows of its banks. Without a sound their bare feet followed the way of other fugitives seeking freedom.

When they reached the riverfront, Caleb led them into the darkness between two small buildings. There he stopped to wait and watch.

As Libby looked out from the shadows, she saw the tall white steamboat owned by her father. *It's still the most beautiful boat on the Mississippi*, Libby thought. She could hardly wait to see Pa. Then he was there, standing next to the gangplank, looking tall and handsome in his captain's uniform.

The waterfront was quiet now, the passengers on board or wherever they wanted to be. The riverbank was empty, as if all the freight that needed to be shipped was on board. But Caleb still waited. And Libby's father still stood near the gangplank, looking upstream as if he was relaxing after a busy day.

Then Pa yawned. Politely he tapped his fingers across his mouth. Turning to the lantern that hung from a nearby post, he blew out the flame.

As Caleb took one step forward, Libby caught a movement nearby. Within the shadow of a nearby warehouse, a deeper shadow moved. Reaching out, Libby put a warning hand on Caleb's arm. Together they edged back, once again hiding between the small buildings.

A moment later a man stepped out from the darkness next to the warehouse. Wearing the red shirt of a lumberjack, he seemed like a stranger. Boldly he walked straight toward the *Christina*. But then Libby recognized him.

"It's Sam McGrady," she whispered.

With Caleb on one side of Libby and Jordan on the other, the three walked forward. Staying a short distance behind Sam, they followed him up the gangplank. Then they closed in behind him.

"Good evening, Captain," McGrady said as though he were a Red Shirt returning from a visit to town.

"Good evening," Captain Norstad replied. "Welcome aboard."

As Pa glanced beyond the man to Libby, McGrady started to slip past him. But Libby spoke up.

"Pa, I'd like you to meet the Stillwater prisoner, Sam McGrady."

As if Libby were out of her mind, Captain Norstad stared at her. "Libby," he began, "do you understand what you're saying?"

To Libby's surprise Sam didn't try to get away. Instead, he looked her father in the eye.

"She's right, Captain. I escaped from the Minnesota Territorial Prison. I want to go back."

"Go back?" Again Captain Norstad stared, this time at Sam McGrady.

But now Sam looked Jordan in the eye. "Your words started eatin' on me."

" 'Cause I said you owes me something?" Jordan asked.

"That, but something else too."

Sam glanced toward Libby. "I heard what you said to her that day on deck. You told her, 'You can't run away from yourself.' It took a while, but I finally figured it out. Trying to run from myself is a whole lot harder than running away from someone else."

Once again Sam faced Captain Norstad. "I don't have the money to buy a ticket up the river. If you take me to Stillwater, I'll go back to prison. If I finish serving my time, I can be with my family again."

"As a changed man?" the captain asked.

"As a changed man," Sam promised. "I won't steal any clothes on the way there."

Captain Norstad stretched out his hand, and Sam McGrady shook on it. Then he looked at Jordan. "You got your freedom. I'm going to get mine."

As Sam McGrady left them, Pa opened his arms to Libby. When they closed around her, she felt warm with love for her father.

"Welcome home, Libby," he said. "Every time you come back, it feels better."

"We're a never-give-up family, aren't we?" Libby said. "We like being together."

Looking down at her, Pa grinned. "I suspect you have a lot to tell me. But I also think your work isn't quite finished. When you get time, why don't you come to my cabin and tell me why I need to buy so many blankets and quilts?"

As Pa started up the stairway, Jordan slipped away. Soon after he disappeared between the buildings near the waterfront, Caleb lit the lantern. Once again he and Libby waited. Again they watched for shadows, movements, and any hidden person. But this time they stood on the deck of the *Christina*.

Finally Caleb lifted the glass of the lantern and blew out the flame. When Jordan and his family started up the gangplank, Libby heard no sound from their bare feet. Without a word Jordan led them around the wide stairs into the cargo room.

Walking forward to the bow of the boat, Libby and Caleb sat down to wait. It wasn't hard for Libby to imagine Jordan pushing aside the machinery near the engine room door. In her mind's eye she saw him pull up the hatch. She saw Serena, Zack, Hattie, and little Rose climb down the ladder. She saw Jordan follow them, holding out a candle to help them find their way into the hiding place. And then Libby imagined Serena and little Rose lying down to sleep on the soft blankets and quilts.

Before long, deckhands brought in the gangplank. As the *Christina* put out into the river, Libby felt relieved. Still she and Caleb waited.

When Jordan didn't come back, Libby knew that his family was safe. Staring up at the moon, Libby felt thankfulness well up within her.

"Is it always like this?" she asked Caleb.

"It's always scary," he said. "And something often goes wrong. But of all the times I've helped someone, this was the hardest."

"Because Jordan needed to go back not far from where he lived?"

"That's part of it. But it was more. I knew how much Jordan's family meant to him."

Far above them the moon shone as brightly as it had the night before. The large paddle wheels slapped the water, and the waves broke against the bow of the *Christina*.

"Libby," Caleb said quietly. "Last night on the ferry, when Jordan paid the fare for his family, I saw you crying."

"I saw you crying too." Libby's voice was soft with remembering.

As though still thinking about Jordan being able to help his family, Caleb reached out and wiped a tear from Libby's cheek. "It's something important we're doing, isn't it?"

Surprised, Libby stared at him, not sure if Caleb was teasing. Then she saw the serious look in his eyes. She remembered how he felt about the midnight rescue. Caleb was not teasing.

"It's something important we're doing," Libby answered. For the rest of her life she would remember Caleb's use of the word *we*.

A Note From Lois

Thanks to each of you who have written to tell me how much you like the ADVENTURES OF THE NORTHWOODS and THE RIVERBOAT ADVENTURES. I enjoy hearing from my readers and feel as though we've become friends through books.

If you would like to receive my newsletter, let me know by writing to

Lois Walfrid Johnson
Bethany House Publishers
11300 Hampshire Ave. S.
Minneapolis, MN 55438

Please include a *stamp* on an *envelope addressed to yourself* for *each* letter you request.

Acknowledgments

Do you ever long to have a real-life hero or heroine? Someone you can look up to and respect? Someone you can admire, not only for what that person has done, but also because of what that person *is*?

I suspect that most of us feel that way. We admire people who care about the beliefs we care about. We respect boys and girls and men and women who take a stand at the right place at the right time, even though it's difficult.

Because of the need for secrecy, we will never know even a tiny fraction of all that happened through the work of the Underground Railroad. Yet we can be sure of one thing: Again and again, fugitive slaves, free blacks, and whites all worked together for one common goal—that not one passenger be lost.

As pioneers poured into southeastern Iowa, its citizens made countless choices that affected the history of the entire state. In the first novel of this series, *Escape Into the Night*, you met some of those history makers—Asa Turner, William Salter, Deacon Trowbridge, the Quakers of Salem, and the Congregational folks of Denmark and Burlington. All of these people risked much in order to live what they believed. Dr. Edwin James of Augusta, Iowa, was another such man.

Though internationally known for his work as a botanist, Dr.

James lived an outwardly quiet life. When his neighbors needed a medical doctor, he helped them without accepting payment. On Sunday mornings he became a pastor. Yet, unknown to many people around him, Dr. James was shaping history.

The case of the fugitive slave named Dick was one of three important slavery trials in southeastern Iowa. In a time when many people were still deciding what they believed about slavery, Dr. James was not afraid to support his beliefs with action.

The third governor of Iowa, James Wilson Grimes, was another man who stood for the freedom of slaves. In writing to his wife about Dick's Burlington trial in 1855, Governor Grimes talked about how few people in Des Moines County had opposed slavery only four years before. According to Grimes, those who expressed such opinions were treated as if they were pickpockets. The court decision about Dick, and the support of one thousand men who made sure that he got safely away, showed the change that had come to the Burlington area within a short period of time.

"Now I am Governor of the State," said Grimes as he wrote about the fugitive slave law. "Three-fourths of the reading and reflecting people of the county agree with me in my sentiments on the law, and a slave could not be returned from Des Moines County into slavery."

Because of the courage of those who lived for what they believed, the opinions of others had changed for good. Those newly formed beliefs shaped history. Yet in many areas of our country, people chose to live what they believed, even when those around them didn't hold the same opinion. The fictional characters, Jonathan and Dorothy Weaver, represent the children and adults who faced different opinions within their own families.

During the Civil War, Missouri was a land and people divided by their beliefs about slavery. In Clark County, Missouri, bitterness and bloodshed split apart entire families. On August 5, 1861, Missouri's northernmost Civil War battle was fought at Athens, only a few miles from where this book is set. In that battle northeastern Missouri was won for the Union. But neighbor fought against neighbor and brother against brother. As Colonel David Moore led his pro-Union troops, two of his sons fought against him.

When the Iowa governor, James Wilson Grimes, became a

United States senator, he took another unpopular stand. President Andrew Johnson was threatened by impeachment, and Senator Grimes chose to protect the Constitution. Though paralyzed by a stroke two days before, he insisted on being carried into the Senate on a stretcher. By his one vote it was decided that a President of the United States could not be removed from office simply because popular opinion went against him. In spite of great personal and political cost, James Wilson Grimes again changed the direction of history.

As you've read, the beautiful countryside of Clark County, Missouri, offered wonderful hideaways for outlaws during the 1850s and 1860s. Horse stealing was a serious problem. David McKee founded the Anti-Horse Thief Association to protect the property of others from theft, and especially from horse thieving. In contrast to groups that took the law into their own hands, the Anti-Horse Thief Association worked with law authorities to bring offenders to justice. By 1916 the group had grown to 50,000 members living in eleven states.

And what about the many escapes from the Minnesota Territorial Prison? A week or so after the time in which Libby, Caleb, and Jordan visited Stillwater, the Territorial legislature decided that the warden should not be held responsible for prisoners if the counties from which they came did not pay for their keep. As a result, some prisoners were set free.

In 1858 prison reform began. Today the Minnesota Correctional Facility—Stillwater is considered a model of modern correctional facilities.

As I think about the writing of this book, I feel humbled by the help I have received from many people. One of these special individuals is Charles L. Blockson, curator of the Afro-American materials at Temple University, Philadelphia, and author of such books as *The Underground Railroad*. Thanks, Charles! At a crucial time you gave me just the encouragement I needed.

My gratitude to the people of Stillwater, Minnesota, one of my long-time favorite towns. Thanks to Kay and Bill Hieb for their willingness to share books and research, as well as showing me their favorite places. Thanks to the editors of the *St. Croix Union*; the Stillwater Public Library and its librarians; the Washington County Historical Society, especially its Warden's House Museum and Arlene Nettekoven and Joan Daniels; historian and writer Brent Peterson, and his and Dean Thilgen's book, *Stillwater: A Photographic History*; Patricia Condon Johnston, *Stillwater: Minnesota's Birthplace*; Anita Albrecht Buck, *Steamboats on the St. Croix*; James Taylor Dunn, *The St. Croix: Midwest Border River*; Chip Kraft, and Nate McGinn. My heartfelt gratitude to long-ago resident and photographer, John Runk, who left a magnificent legacy for all of us.

Thanks also to my new friend, Kyle Raph; Helmar Heckel for the right word at the right time; Joe Hansen, gifted Northern Kentucky University Elderhostel leader; James Glover and Walter Johnson for their great help with horses and wagons; long-time dog-lovers Tom Robinson, president of the Minnesota Valley Kennel Club, and Norma Robinson, president of the Newfoundland Dog Club of the Greater Twin Cities, Eagan, Minnesota.

In Burlington, Iowa, thanks to Susie Guest, library assistant, Burlington Free Public Library; Anna Martin, historian, and the historical board of the First Congregational Church; and the Burlington *Hawk Eye*. My gratitude to Gayla Young, Denmark, Iowa; Gerald Thele, Weaver, Iowa; Hazelle and Clay Lanman for their tour of the Pearson House, Keosauqua, Iowa; and the *Des Moines Register*.

Again I am indebted to Robert L. Miller, curator of a national historic landmark, the steamer *George M. Verity*, Keokuk River Museum, Keokuk, Iowa. In addition to the museum resources, Bob has shared of his own personal knowledge and read portions of the manuscript. For this novel, thanks, also, to Bob's wife, Margaret Miller, and their son, John Miller.

The village called *Cahoka* in this novel is now spelled *Kahoka*. Thanks to the Clark County Historical Society, their Kahoka museum, and to society president, Raymond Morrow; to the editors of the incredible special edition for Clark County's Old Settlers 100th Celebration; Linda Brown-Kubisch, reference librarian, State Historical Society of Missouri at Columbia; the Hannibal Public Library; and the Hannibal *Tri-Weekly Messenger*.

Roberta and Hurley Hagood, Hannibal historians and authors of such wonderful books as *The Story of Hannibal, Hannibal, Too*, and *Hannibal Yesterdays*, once again shared freely of their research and time. In addition to providing background information they answered countless questions and read a portion of the manuscript.

Thanks to you, Paul and Lucille Herron, for sharing your wonderful, pre-Civil War farm home with us. Your inspiration helped the story of Jordan's family and the Weaver family come alive.

My deep gratitude to my artist, Andrea Jorgenson, who has illustrated ten Adventures of the Northwoods novels and now three Riverboat Adventures. It's been a great partnership, Andrea! Thanks to my in-house editors—Rochelle Glöege, Natasha Sperling, and Janna Anderson—and the entire Bethany team.

Three special people have helped to shape my thinking for this book. My husband Roy has offered his wisdom and love for kids, as well as his daily encouragement. Our son Kevin has shared and lived that same love for young people. Ron Klug, my faithful, courageous, fire-eating editor, has waded through the early stages of this book, suggested scenes I would have forgotten, and made sure that all the things I wanted to tell you have come together in the story you read.

Finally, to all of you who have cared about me, both as a person and as a writer, thank you!